Seek a Safe Harbor

Seek a Safe Harbor

Women of Monterey, Book 1

Marilyn Read
Cheryl Spears Waugh

Tranquility Press, 2019

For information:
Tranquility Press
723 W University Ave #300-234
Georgetown TX 78626
TranquilityPress.Net
TranquilityPress@gmail.com

This book is a work of fiction. Historical figures are used fictitiously, and any scenes, situations, incidents or dialogue concerning them are not to be inferred as real. Any other similarity to real persons, living or dead, is entirely coincidental and not intended by the authors.

Cover design: Ken Raney, KenRaney.com

ISBN: 978-1-950481-01-9
PCN: 2019935625

Publisher's Cataloging-in-Publication data

Names: Read, Marilyn, author. | Waugh, Cheryl Spears, author.
Title: Seek a safe harbor / by Marilyn Read and Cheryl Spears Waugh.
Series: Women of Monterey.
Description: Georgetown, TX: Tranquility Press, 2019.
Identifiers: LCCN 2019935625 |
ISBN 978-1-950481-01-9 (paperback) | ISBN 978-1-950481-04-0 (e-Book)
Subjects: LCSH Mission San Carlos Borromeo (Carmel, Calif.)--History--Fiction. | Franciscans--Missions--California--History--Fiction. | Missions, Spanish--California--History--Fiction. | Indians of North America--Missions--California--History--Fiction. | Man-woman relationships--Fiction. | Family--Fiction. | BISAC FICTION / Historical / General
Classification: LCC PS3618.E2242 S44 2019 | DDC 813.6--dc23

To Kerri and Alleen,
who in their lives and deaths showed us
that when we follow God's commands
the wisdom we seek is right at hand.

Part 1: Anna
Seek a Safe Harbor

One

June 1783, Rancho de Arista
San Luis Obispo, Spanish Alta California

Footsteps echoed in the hacienda's tiled entry hall. Her own? Or was he behind her—stalking her, mocking her state of nerves? Anna Arista forced herself to stop and glance over her shoulder. Her breath slipped out between the fingers she'd placed over her mouth. Porfirio wasn't there.

Three years of such treatment from her brother since their parents' deaths. Anna offered a wordless prayer. If things went well today, she'd be free of her only sibling's oppressive guardianship; if not, she could lose everything. His reckless wagers could cost them the very roof over their head.

The early morning bite of toast and swallow of coffee did little to soothe her stomach six hours later. Anna's thoughts scurried this way and that. She clutched the silver crucifix at her throat and whispered the words Father had often said. "*God is always near.*

Give thanks even when things are wrong."

Resisting the urge to pace again, Anna pressed her forehead against a front window pane. Through the uneven surface of the glass came faint notes of a bird's song and the liquid gurgle of the stone fountain. The beloved adobe ranch house had been her home from birth. Father, one of the first noblemen to come to Alta California, had built it on a land grant from Spain's king. But the property now belonged to Porfirio and nothing was certain any more.

A ragged sigh escaped. A woman needed a protector. Like Father had been for Mamá. A decisive man who would take control of affairs and provide a life of ease and certainty.

She dreamed of him. Strong and tender. Sensitive to her need for protection. "Forever," he would whisper as he took her up with him onto a black stallion. They would gallop away from Porfirio and all his problems— forever sharing a love like her parents. She would never be lonely again.

Anna straightened her shoulders. Today she must face the real men in her life. Porfirio, her profligate brother, and Pedro Madrigal, the man Father had chosen for her. Perhaps not her choice, but honor thy father. *Californios* clung to the old ways, marrying their daughters to sons of other aristocrats in betrothals arranged by parents. Father believed he'd assured her future in the society of landed Californios by providing her with a generous dowry. And that was the problem. Porfirio's uncontrolled gambling had frittered it away.

Her stomach tightened. Pedro had requested this afternoon's meeting with her and Porfirio. What would come of it?

In accordance with Spanish custom, she and Pedro did not have influence over the betrothal, nor had they spent time together without a chaperone. Pedro was a sweet friend in her life, not a romantic lover. Romantic feelings had little to do with it. Truth be told, it was more a matter of choosing a mate of equal fortune and social standing. The system had worked well for hundreds of years and it would work for her—if Porfirio had not already ruined everything.

Plans were proceeding unhindered until that horrible week when Father and Mamá died of influenza. They were with God, and she was here, trying to hold together what was left of Father's fortune.

Another peek showed the curved drive still empty and no carriage beyond the gate. Perhaps Pedro had changed his mind and decided there was nothing to discuss. The wedding would proceed on schedule.

Please, Holy Father, let it be so. They could have a good marriage. And Pedro was her only hope for continuing a familiar life. If he cast her aside, no other—

Anna whirled as Porfirio strode into the entry, immaculate as always, the ever-present glass of brandy in his hand.

"I've been thinking, *hermana*."

Her empty stomach knotted. Whenever Porfirio called her *sister*, he wanted something. He usually ignored family ties in favor of reminding her that she was his legal ward for another two years and a drain on their dwindling finances.

"And?" she prompted. Her voice sounded thin, too high for a woman of nineteen. She cleared her throat.

"Your fears may be correct. If Pedro comes to

11

set aside your betrothal, you must demand a large monetary settlement. You owe me some effort to pay for your keep." Porfirio brushed at a speck on his jacket. "You know how to persuade him. Flash your big green eyes and toss that golden hair. Or promise to see him even after the break."

Anna wanted to stamp her foot, but highborn women did not indulge in strong emotion. She stared out the window, pretending to study Porfirio's proposal. How dare he? A monetary demand was beneath her. She had her pride. And what of the large dowry Father provided? The fortune would have kept her for a lifetime, were it not for his reckless gambling.

Her chest began to ache. Oh, for the days when Father was strong and well. When his sailing ships brought all manner of goods to Alta California and *Rancho Arista* offered lavish gatherings. Days when Anna laughed and danced, the apple of her parents' adoring and watchful eyes.

A sudden clatter of hoofbeats and jingle of harness announced a coach's arrival. Anna touched her crucifix and glanced at her brother.

"*Bueno.*" Porfirio emptied his glass. "Remember your obligation, *hermana.*" He disappeared behind the *salón's* heavy redwood doors on the far side of the entry hall. He would wait for her, all the while brooding about how to use her relationship with Pedro to his advantage.

Anna coaxed her fingers from her cross. Face this predicament with grace. Pedro was kind and devoted. If he dissolved the betrothal, the fault lay with Porfirio.

A knock sounded. Pedro could wait while she gathered her resolve. She checked her reflection in the hall mirror and pinched her pale cheeks.

The role of a rancher's wife would come naturally. She, not Porfirio, had spent hours in the saddle with Father, riding ranges and watching *vaqueros* train blooded stallions.

If she couldn't live in this house, she wanted one like it, with walls that smelled of the earth. One with long hallways and a tiled roof where doves gathered in the evening. Children playing in the courtyard. The life she'd been bred to live.

Mamá said love often developed after marriage. Put away her fancies of heart-pulsing romance and offer Pedro the devotion a husband deserved—if she still had a choice.

A second knock sent Anna hurrying toward the entrance. She smoothed her bodice and tugged open the door. No *mayordomo* these days to usher guests into the hacienda. Faithful Sebastiano was too old to be on his feet all day and a younger man would expect a stipend and better living quarters.

"I've missed you, Pedro," Anna said. His troubled brown gaze slid away. He rubbed the back of his neck and twisted his ring. His replies to questions about his mother and sister were, however, reassuring. And he managed a weak smile.

"Porfirio is waiting."

Pedro's smile died and his forehead wrinkled. He cleared his throat and offered his arm, but didn't look at her. Anna led the way to the *salón*, head held high, and met Porfirio's hard gaze. He almost sneered. Pedro's arm began to tremble beneath her hand and she fought for breath. Her worst fear was true. He meant to set her aside.

Minutes later, he neared the end of his lengthy disavowal and she realized why Pedro Madrigal had never engaged her heart. Not because he bore traces of recurring illness in his spare frame and lackluster hair, nor because his eyes were too close together. Looks were unimportant. He was a man of faith and he had a sweet nature. Character was what one looked for in a mate, Father said. But a woman needed a strong man — one who could protect her. Pedro was not that man.

"My father has made his wishes clear, Anna. There can be no marriage. If there were any way —" His eyes begged for forgiveness. The color had drained from his face and his mouth twisted. Pedro's voice trailed away and he glanced toward Porfirio.

Anna coughed to cover a sniff. *Don't worry, Pedro. My brother is not an outraged protector ready to pound you into the tiles.*

Porfirio cast a scornful glance and turned his back. Pedro fidgeted and Anna prayed. Surely her brother would at least try to make a persuasive argument; but he turned to her.

"Anna?" he prompted.

Her breath caught in her throat. What should she do? Porfirio could be cruel when she opposed him, and Pedro's wealthy father could well afford a settlement. But even if Don Madrigal agreed to pay, she would never benefit. Reckless wagers or old debts would soon drain the new resources.

Pedro's sweating brow and anxious eyes made him look pitiful. She laid her hand on his arm. "We understand. You have no choice." His tortured expression prompted her to add, "I will see you out. Please give my love to your dear mother and sister."

Porfirio's gaze speared hers and he raised an eyebrow. A small smile curved his lips, more unsettling than a show of anger.

Anna's knees weakened with the click of the door. When Pedro had stood beside her, pride and a sense of fairness overrode her fear of Porfirio's reprisal. Now Pedro was gone and she had to face her brother alone. She was hardly aware of walking back to the *salón*.

His back to her, Porfirio stirred the embers of a meager fire. Anna tucked her arms around her body to stop its trembling. If only Father were here to deal with Porfirio's weakness and scheming. She cleared her throat. "We knew it would come to this."

He stopped for a moment; then continued stabbing at the smoldering back log. The silence lengthened.

"I understand your distress, *hermano*," she continued, "but Father begged us to remain committed to each other and to the ranch. The ships are gone, but we must preserve the hacienda. It's Father's legacy. I'll do all I can to help."

Porfirio racked the poker. Legs apart, shoulders erect in his swordsman's stance, he watched her. His eyes were granite chips, gray and cold.

"Exactly what can you offer in aid of my distress, as you characterize present circumstances? Without protest you allowed the only asset you held in this world to walk out the door. Even Pedro recognized you as a useless ornament and tired of you." Porfirio refilled his glass and returned to the fire.

The words stung, but they were nothing new. Anna stood taller. He created the crisis. Let him find another solution.

Porfirio's lip curled. "Pedro no doubt came prepared with a generous offer. His father would have paid handsomely for your cooperation, but you allowed him to wriggle away unscathed."

"Unscathed? Did you not see his misery?" She crossed to Porfirio's side and touched his arm. He wouldn't look at her. "I acted as Father would have wished. I did the thing that honors God."

He turned and stared at her. Had Father's words pierced his self-concern? She hurried on, "Together we can—"

Porfirio pressed a finger to her mouth. "Hush, Anna." He kissed her forehead. "Your wayward sympathy will cost you. I will correct your misplaced loyalty. In fact, a resolution may be on its way." He left without a backward glance.

Anna stamped her foot.

Two

Two days later, Porfirio hailed Anna in the courtyard as she returned from an afternoon's ride. He helped her dismount. Jauntiness in his step betrayed his mood. Anna swallowed her irritation. If only he'd let her be.

Her brother grinned. "Good news! Your future is arranged and I'm free to chart a course out of misfortune."

"Arranged without consulting me?" Fire ignited in Anna's core and she sought her crucifix.

Porfirio scowled. "I'm willing to see you into a good start, but success will be up to you. Father's not here to cater to his favorite child."

As he continued his litany of Father's unfair treatment, her attention wandered. She'd heard it all before.

Porfirio had always resented her bond with Father. Why couldn't he see Father had loved him just as much? And Mamá had indulged him, protecting him from Father's discipline. Perhaps that was Porfirio's problem. He'd become used to a pampered life without consequences. His next words made clear to her it no longer mattered.

"You have no choice but to agree to my decision. I will accept no further responsibility for care of an indigent sister."

"I'm indigent because you've made me so. This is unfair, Porfirio. Cruel."

He continued as if she hadn't spoken. "It will take every penny I can scrape up to maintain the pretense of a lifestyle that might attract a wealthy, if lamentably older, widow. I plan to go to Mexico City for the search."

"Take me with you. I can return to the convent."

"Not likely, Anna. I'll have to sail on a merchant ship. Even that small fare is a burden."

With his looks and the charm he could turn on at will, he would succeed in Mexico. Here, her lost dowry denied her the possibility of serious suitors among the sons of aristocrats, and lesser men would be intimidated by her social standing. She had only Porfirio, and he wanted no part of her. Unfair, but the way of the world. Women had little say in determining the course of their lives.

Anna tightened her grip on the riding crop. "So then? Have you decided to send me to Majorca?" If she could not have the sanctuary and security offered by the Mexican convent, Father's distant family offered her hope. Surely they would welcome her.

Porfirio plucked a rose, sniffed it, and offered it to her with a flourish. "Listen closely, Anna. I said I have a solution. Father would be pleased to learn those boring stories of his friar friend were not wasted on me. I sent word to Fray Junipero Serra." His expression was triumphant.

Fray Serra? How could he possibly help her?

"The humble friend of Father's boyhood has risen to the position of President of all California Missions. Can you believe it? The one who walks wherever he goes? I never thought he'd amount to anything, but he is now a man of great influence."

Father had spoken often of his childhood friend from Majorca. They'd grown up together but gone in very separate ways. His stories of Fray Serra often bordered on hero worship. Porfirio would never understand a man who could choose the good of others above his own.

Anna swallowed hard. *Am I not also overly concerned with comfort and a life of plenty? I can't lose it. It's all I know.*

"Father always believed in Fray Serra. His humility was one of the qualities Father admired most. That and his concern for people. But what has that to do with me?"

Porfirio sneered. "Well, apparently his concern extends to the daughter of his boyhood friend. He has invited you to come north to Mission San Carlos de Borromeo at Monterey Bay. Fray Serra has found employment for you. You will be nurse-companion to the invalid wife of the owner of a vast ranch near the mission—León de Montaraz."

Anna gasped. Employment! She couldn't tend her own needs, much less those of an invalid. Porfirio's cold stare told her he knew full well the impact of his words.

Her head spun and she sought a bench. *Wait a moment.*

She glared up at Porfirio. "How could you arrange this in two days? Monterey is a hard four or five days' ride up the coast." Porfirio's gaze shifted. "Your gambling cronies warned you of a broken engagement, ¿Verdad? It's true, isn't it?"

His smirk offered a grudging compliment to her quick deduction. Anna didn't try to hide her distaste. "Any amount I received from Pedro would have changed nothing. The moment my dowry was gone, my fate was settled." Heat mounted to her cheeks and she fought the urge to strike him. Proper young ladies did not indulge in aggression.

Porfirio laughed and wagged his finger. "Careful, Anna. Temper."

Her voice shook. "You dangled false hope in front of me and then savored my agony over a choice which didn't exist."

His glittering gaze showed it was true. Porfirio enjoyed watching her struggle. No surprise; there'd never been brotherly love in that cold heart.

Anna's blood alternated hot and cold. *I will rise above the fury welling up inside. Mamá instilled in me the grace to—*

Anna slapped Porfirio's gloating face with all the strength she could muster. Time slowed as he went rigid. She didn't enjoy inflicting pain, so why did her stinging hand feel so good?

A dark flush suffused Porfirio's neck and face. He stared at her and then rubbed his cheek as the moment lengthened. What would he do?

She watched in disbelief as a slow smile curved his lips. He shook his head and wagged his finger again. "Shame on you. Conduct unbefitting a lady, Anna.

What would Mamá say?"

He was laughing at her! Porfirio didn't care enough about his own sister to be angry with her. If she were not so incensed, she would pity him.

"You may have destroyed my chances here among families of reputation, but I will go to Majorca." She raised her chin. "Father's family cannot be as callous as you."

"And how will you pay your way?" He sniffed. "I doubt Father's relations will offer another loan to anyone in this house. Their generosity goes only so far and I found their limit."

He pursed his lips. The imprint of her hand still glowed on his cheek. "Your choices are few, *hermana*. Possibly Fray Serra can find use for you at the Mission if you turn down the position with de Montaraz. Or you can join an order. Face your future with the courage and determination I employ." He sounded bored and ready to terminate the encounter.

"Courage? Determination? In the meeting with Pedro, you showed neither." Porfirio's satisfied smile stopped her. Accusations would gain her nothing. He reveled in emotional scenes. She held back a sob. No tears in front of him.

He shrugged with a finality Anna found chilling. "Accept Fray Serra's offer as the godsend it is. I'll send Carlita to help you pack."

She couldn't simply fold like a wilted rose. "I require a *chaperona*. A woman of good reputation does not travel without a suitable female companion."

Another shrug. "And who will pay for this *chaperona*? You? Sebastiano has offered to accompany you since he traveled to Monterey years ago with

Father. In fact, he insists." Porfirio ambled away toward the house.

As infuriating as it was, he was right. Her choices were few. A lady's companion was a step above household service, but employment, however genteel, decreed death to her dream of marriage to a man of standing. She'd be far from home and among strangers.

Still, she was educated and Father had always said she had a good head on her shoulders and a heart for God. In Monterey perhaps she could start anew, however difficult it might be. She must swallow her pride and go into service. Her dream man was nowhere in sight.

The small carriage Porfirio assigned didn't offer space for many of her belongings. Anna refused to join Carlita's weeping bouts as she and her maid packed over the next two days. She chose which treasured possessions to leave behind, finding space for her mother's prayer book and mementos of her father. She reread Father's letters from Fray Serra, then stowed them in the reticule that would remain with her in the coach.

Porfirio was closing the house to depart for Mexico. She had no home. Her one consolation was Sebastiano. Father's retired valet would accompany her on the trip up the California coast from San Luis Obispo to Monterey. Father would approve. He'd trusted Sebastiano as he had few men.

His health was failing. It would be a difficult journey for both of them, but she clung to his offer in gratitude. At least she would have a familiar face.

Since her childhood, Sebastiano had offered his loving regard.

Before sunrise, he handed her into the coach. Over her protests he took his accustomed place outside and Anna waved to a sobbing Carlita. Porfirio had offered his farewell the previous night when he'd pressed a gold coin into her hand. "All I can spare, Anna."

An aging footman and a gold coin were all that protected her on the long road to Monterey. She'd chosen the only option that made sense. So why the creeping shadow at the edge of her mind? The feeling that she'd just made the worst decision of her life?

Anna fingered her silver crucifix, Father's gift at her confirmation. "To remind you God is always with you, Anna." God and Father felt far away—as far as heaven from earth. Tears she had denied in the past few days blurred her last view of Hacienda Arista.

Three

Monterey Bay, Alta California

Sebastiano helped Anna from the carriage. "Your introduction to Monterey Bay, Señorita. I wanted it to be from this hill near the fort. Look at the surf from this height."

"Four bone-jarring days of travel—one through a windstorm—but we've arrived. And the view *is* magnificent."

Anna's gaze caught a wind-swept curve of coast with a few off-shore islands that brought to mind ships anchored afar. The sun was sinking down behind the horizon.

"Incredible, Sebastiano. Waves like rows of white-capped soldiers pressing toward their fate on the sand."

The sea air's salty tang filled her lungs and raucous cries of seagulls assaulted her ears as they swarmed and wheeled in endless competition for food. One brushed briefly along the top of a swell before reeling high above her. Holding out her arms, she whirled around.

"Exhilarating." The backbone of ancient mountains stretched as far as she could see in either direction. Trees of fantastic shapes rose from cliffs above the sea, twisted and flat-topped by centuries of strong winds. According to one of Fray Serra's letters, these cypress trees were saplings at the time of Christ's birth.

A sailing vessel entered the harbor in full rig, sails billowing, with the sea breaking before its bow. How many times had she watched Father return from a voyage? Tears blurred her eyes. She wanted to run headlong across the sand to meet him.

Sebastiano touched her arm. "Courage, *pequeña*."

Little one. Anna did feel small looking at this endless coastline and contemplating the staggering changes in her future.

He gestured toward the few squat buildings and wooden palisades that frowned over an otherwise breathtaking scene. "The Royal Presidio of San Carlos de Monterey, founded along with the mission. We visited it when I came years ago with your father."

Anna dabbed her eyes with Sebastiano's kerchief and manufactured a smile. "King Carlos might withdraw any mention of royalty in its name if he could see it."

Sebastiano smiled. "Surprising they have not improved the fort since our visit eight years ago. Spanish sailors knew about the bay for two hundred years before Fray Serra came, but none had explored it. He stood here in his peasant's sandals and claimed the land for God and the church."

In peasant's sandals. The humble beginning Porfirio had scorned. Fray Serra had come to a wilderness in order to serve God. Had God drawn her here, as well? Could she learn to serve the Lord as Fray Serra had done?

The thought frightened her. Fray Serra's purpose must have been clear and he'd been prepared to follow. She'd been forced into this land. Could she set aside her grief and worries to begin again?

"It's growing late, Sebastiano. I could linger, but I suppose we must go. Fold your tall body back into that tiny carriage." He'd finally consented to ride inside with her.

He laughed. "It feels like I wear that rolling box."

From the coast they turned northeast to a road along the Carmel River. Anna was eager to see the mission. It should be imposing. Monterey was the capital of Alta California and Mission San Carlos de Borromeo was the headquarters for Fray Serra, the President of all the missions.

When the coach rattled into a cobble-stoned quadrangle, the rosy glow from a vanished sun still washed the sky. Anna saw small buildings made of adobe. None of the glory of Spanish stone construction.

"I expected a stone church."

"These friars are Alcantarines, a reformed order of Franciscans who keep to strict vows of poverty. One day they may build a fine mission to God's glory, but for now they live as their converts do."

Topped by a wooden cross, the chapel was roofed in clay tiles, but several other buildings had thatched roofs. A young, red-haired friar stood in the chapel's open door. He raised his hand and waved, then turned and hurried away in the direction of some small huts.

An immense wooden cross towered near the church. It was not the familiar Roman cross of Anna's crucifix. This one had two crossbars, one atop the upright.

"An unusual cross, Sebastiano."

"Fray Serra told us its story. Shaped like a Greek *T*. Saint Francis of Assisi, the Franciscan founder, claimed it as his crest. A picture of Christ, he said, its arms outstretched to embrace the leper and the outcast."

"Appropriate," Anna murmured. Something fluttered inside and she touched her crucifix. She would soon meet the man who held her future. "Father admired Fray Serra as he did no other. Said he was the Father of California. I'm intimidated by the thought of meeting him."

"A man of purpose, but approachable. You will see." Sebastiano smiled. "When he entered the order, Fray Serra chose the name of one of Saint Francis' most humble companions, Brother Juniper."

Reassuring, but would the friar see her as an interruption to his busy life? A burden, as Porfirio did? She raised her chin. She would not allow Porfirio's poor estimation to color her thinking. God loved her. That should be enough.

She vowed to carry that thought with her, but her heart pounded as she awaited her first glimpse of the friar. Father had described him only as a small man with a stern face and a lion's heart.

As the coach stopped, excited voices filled the air. Natives of all ages hurried to greet them. They pressed so close that the driver had to wave them back. Sebastiano steadied Anna down the step.

Muscle-stiffening hours of travel were behind her. Anna clung to her old friend's arm and looked up at his lined face and tired eyes. His white hair shone as a badge to years of faithful service. She patted his hand.

"Thank you for delivering me to my new life, Sebastiano. I'll sorely miss your friendship." She ducked her head to hide tears. "Let's see if we can find Father Serra."

Fray Serra, however, found them. The crowd parted before a graying man dressed in a hooded tunic with a knotted white cord at his waist. A man of sharp features, he stood scant inches above Anna's five feet. He limped toward them in worn sandals.

He was older than Father and every year had left its mark. One of his feet looked swollen and inflamed, but his serene face welcomed them. A little forelock of hair centered his upper forehead. It drew Anna's attention to the friar's deep-set brown eyes and thin, straight nose.

"Señorita Arista. Anna, how welcome you are! A sight to my aging eyes." He studied her face. "I see characteristics of your dear father, but your beauty is that of your Castilian mother. Her green eyes and golden hair."

He greeted Sebastiano as Anna curtsied, mindful of Mamá's careful training. Fray Serra steadied her rise. "You come to me in a new endeavor, Anna, and your father would approve. As youngsters on the Island of Mallorca, Rodrigo thought I would miss out on adventure if I pursued a religious life, but he came to understand what fulfillment I have found in following a Savior who calls us to the unknown."

Surely God did not plan all that had happened

to her: the deaths of her parents in the same week and the frustrating years of watching Porfirio fritter away their livelihood. Sands beneath her feet seemed to have shifted. Without the steadying influence of her parents, would she ever find solid ground again?

She studied the serene features of Fray Serra. His letters revealed he had driven himself from Mexico to California, from one mission to the next—exhorting, baptizing, confirming. She could see little of the weariness that must characterize the friar's days. He appeared confident and strong. Had he ever felt lost and alone?

He directed the young red-haired priest at his side to take Sebastiano and the coach driver to lodging. "Come with me, Anna. You can refresh yourself before we dine. You must be tired."

Tears dewed her lashes. Here stood a man who suffered continual hardship, yet he was concerned for her comfort. "Blessed Father Serra, your very presence restores me. I am thankful for your protection. In your presence I feel God is surely with me."

Fray Serra's eyebrows rose. "He *is*, Anna. Always."

Her accommodation for the night was an austere cell much like the one at Mission San Antonio de Padua where she had slept two evenings earlier. It held a cot and a table with a candle and chair. The friars accepted privation as part of their service and shared what they had.

Anna and Fray Serra had dinner with three other friars on location: Friar Peralta, the young red-haired priest, and two older men. One of them was writing a history of Franciscan efforts in California. He offered to conduct the Angelus service of evening devotions, leaving Fray Serra free to talk with Anna.

The friar led Anna to his small hut. The porch held four rustic but surprisingly comfortable chairs. He wasted no time.

"Anna, your father confided in me his concern for your brother's character. When Porfirio's message arrived, I realized Rodrigo's fears were well founded. Hence my offer. We need not speak of your brother unless you wish."

"Thank you. What happened was painful, but I cannot dwell on it."

His stillness was extraordinary. A sense of peace stole over Anna. Muscles relaxed for the first time in days. Serene minutes passed.

"Are you frightened by your circumstances?"

When she admitted she was filled with uncertainty, Fray Serra nodded. "You can remain here with us and serve at the mission teaching children. More than a hundred we have now. Such joy to see those little ones clothed and to hear them singing praises in the Spanish language."

Anna's heart lifted. She wasn't sure about dealing with children, but perhaps it would be better to stay at the mission. Fray Serra waited for her to deliberate, seconds stretching into minutes as Anna gazed at the *tau* cross.

"Trust God," Father's voice whispered within. Was God opening a door for her?

"You will be protected with us, Anna, just as a ship in the harbor is safe. But, as your father well knew, that is not why ships are created."

But a ship is built to withstand wild seas. I've known

only calm waters and comfort for most of my life. I fear storms and uncertainty.

Fray Serra's peaceful voice cut short her wavering. "Ours is a life of hardship for a young woman used to gentility. At Rancho de Montaraz you will be among people of culture and have the company of a woman not unlike your mother, although younger."

A woman like Mamá? That sounded like the answer to prayers.

"What would they expect of me, Father?" Her words opened the door. The decision was made.

Four

The day was dying. A breeze freshened and Anna detected a tang of salt. Voices in song arose from the chapel. Her question hung in the air. According to Father, wise people spoke only after careful thought or prayer.

"Doña de Montaraz looks forward to your companionship. The two of you should get along well. Don León will be glad to find an educated companion for his wife. I believe they offer much that we cannot, but the decision must be yours. Your father would have wished it so."

Anna tried to sound confident. "Please tell me a little more of my prospective employers. Are there children?"

"No children. Doña Juliana is, I believe, a few years older than her husband, who nears thirty years of age. She had frail health when the couple married and has steadily declined. Don León worries also about her mental state."

Alarming.

"What does that mean? I have no nursing experience."

"She is a nervous, impetuous woman. Your calm manner should reassure her. Perhaps you can find ways to increase her appetite and see that she takes gentle exercise. Keep her mentally active. Don León believes she has begun sleeping too much."

"Surely he has in mind more requirements of a companion for his wife. I may be unable to fulfill his expectations."

"Of course, you do not have the wisdom or ability." Fray Serra's eyes twinkled. "Prayer is where our fears go to die, Anna. We drag them out one by one and stand them before God. Courage does not panic—it prays."

She smiled. "I do tend to wring my hands in each new crisis, but I try not to let it show."

Fray Serra studied her. He must realize how frightened she was. *Can words help, no matter how wise they are?*

"Remember, Anna. God equips the called, but not until they are in the midst of the fray."

His gentle wit was surprising, but Fray Serra did not smile. "These missions would not exist if I'd been the one to ensure their success. They would have failed miserably if founded on my wisdom. I can tell you, God *is* the answer to every need."

Anna nodded and managed a smile. *But you had years of study and training behind you. I had only Father and Mamá's guidance, and now they are gone.*

"The first year my compatriot and I registered only twenty baptisms," he said. "From the beginning we emphasized the importance of communication.

With our God, between the two of us, and with our congregants. At the end of the first year, we had four big boys who were able to say their prayers, and making other progress in the Castilian tongue. I was learning from them the language of this country."

Willing to learn from children. His humility touched her. But what did it have to do with her?

"Each mission is surrounded by native peoples who speak a different dialect, so we establish a common idiom: Spanish. However, I insist that my friars learn the speech of the people at each of the soon-to-be nine missions that line the coast of Alta California. Communication is the key, Anna."

Anna looked away from his earnest intensity. What was he talking about? Would an older, sophisticated woman—especially one whose mental state was impaired—accept her ideas?

She blurted out, "What can Doña de Montaraz possibly want to hear from a paid servant more than ten years her junior?" She caught a breath as her cheeks heated. "Oh, I am sorry—"

"Listen and watch her actions. Pray to discern the true meaning of what both of your employers say."

She forced a nod. "I believe in prayer." But most of hers had gone unanswered. *I prayed so hard for Father and Mamá to get well. And I prayed that Pedro would go through with the marriage.*

"We pray to receive God Himself, not what He can give to us. Pray to know Him, resemble Him, love Him, and to delight in Him."

"Then I am not sure I even know how to pray," she confessed. "It seems I am always asking."

"God wants us to ask. And then He wants us

to listen and wait for His answer. Though it may not meet our expectations, it is always what we need." He paused, his gaze boring into hers. She was in the presence of God's wisdom. "God is sending you as a gift of His grace."

"A humbling and thoroughly frightening commission," she murmured. She studied the floor as her mind churned with the friar's challenges. How she needed to believe God would help her. She was so unskilled. But at least she would be with people who led a life similar to the one now lost to her. It wouldn't be peasant sandals and privation. She cringed from the unworthy thought. How weak she was.

"Stay close to Him, Anna, with His precepts ever before you. It's easy to lose God's way in the midst of luxury. My job is made much simpler by my vows of poverty."

Perhaps she feared poverty most of all. Anna lifted her face to his and read determination there. In the small, aging man she sensed a commitment and faith far beyond her own.

"I pray you will find a kindred faith in Señora de Montaraz. A way shared is easier, but a solitary one is not impossible. Obedience is your only protection. Never look back. Only forward with God. He will guide you."

She wanted to ask, "But how can I obey if I cannot hear His voice?" She was as lacking at recognizing Divine guidance as she was at caring for an invalid.

He patted her arm. "Now you must rest, my daughter. *Matines,* our morning devotions, are at dawn."

Her confidence had not increased with Fray

Serra's counsel. Sleep eluded her. How could the friars sleep on the hard, narrow cots? The straw mattress given her as a guest now lay on the floor. Its odor reminded her of a barn.

She rose and opened her door, stepped outside, and leaned against the adobe wall. Warmed by the still-present heat of a vanished sun, she stared up at a sky filled with stars. Father said God guided sailors by the positions of certain stars. She had no star to lead her.

Fray Serra's wise words about prayer and listening seemed beyond her. Almost a foreign language. One she longed to learn, but seemingly impossible. She was on her own.

Hacienda de Montaraz was the only choice that made sense. Even Fray Serra thought it best. It offered a far easier life than the mission school. How could she teach children when she had no answers? And then there was her pride. At least she would be among people whose motives she understood.

Father had great pride in his Majorcan heritage. He always said an endeavor once begun must be completed with honor. She *would* succeed. She was Father's daughter, not the useless ornament of Porfirio's estimation.

The following morning Anna watched Sebastiano help the aging friar into the carriage. Fray Serra murmured, "I ride in the interest of saving time. I prefer to walk in the way of Jesus, but failing legs require me to ride more often than I like."

She sneaked a glance at his swollen foot and looked up to note that Sebastiano's face reflected her own concern. He handed her into the coach opposite the padre and took his place outside.

Questions raced through Anna's mind, but she respected the friar's silence and his closed eyes. It gave her time to rehearse phrases for her prospective employers. Besides, Father had often said, "Men think best in silence."

Anna concentrated on preparing for the interview, but after a few moments she shook her head. Her inexperience would show. She must pretend to be prepared. Act confident without exaggerating her abilities. She couldn't let this opportunity elude her. It was the best offer she would have.

"The four miles have gone quickly, sitting in the comfort of this coach," Fray Serra said. "You can see the house from your window. A comfortable one, but Don León has plans to triple its footprint." Fray Serra shook his head. "Always seeking perfection."

Anna's mouth went dry. *Perfection? I don't have a chance.* A man filled with plans, and accustomed to competence from the many employees it must take to operate this vast ranch. Used to the best, he would surely expect more than she could offer. She had nothing to recommend her but Fray Serra's belief in the certainty of God's guidance. If only her faith matched the friar's.

The coach lurched to a stop and Sebastiano's face showed at the window, looking as sad as Anna felt. She waited for him to open her door a last time. When her feet were on the ground, she put her arms around his neck.

"Words fail me, dear friend. You will be forever a treasured memory. You loved my father, and since I can remember, you have loved me."

"Fray Serra will see to your welfare, Anna. I do not believe I could leave you in the hands of a better man."

"*Vaya con Diós,* Sebastiano. Go with God." She turned away before tears spilled.

Anna looked around and saw her old home—as it had been in better days. Her heart lifted. She could be happy here. Trees spread shade inside an earthen fence surrounding a large structure of brown adobe. Its red tiled roof was lined with a muted rainbow of pigeon doves, their mournful calls answering others atop the fence and in garden trees.

An *arcada,* a long, arched porch floored in quarry tiles, spanned the length of the house. Pots of flowering plants and a stone fountain filled the air with inviting scents and sounds.

Yet Don León de Montaraz plans a more imposing house. Anna drew a deep breath. She could, she *would,* succeed. She wanted to live here. It was the house of her dreams. Not *her* house, but she could enjoy all it offered.

Fray Serra offered his arm and the two stepped through one of the archways, pausing to look around. "A lovely garden, Anna. You and Doña Juliana will enjoy strolls here."

Near the gate Anna spied a large cypress like those of the coast and the mission. In a far corner, a mature cedar elm's limbs swept so low that one burrowed into the soil. Chirps of birds and insects hinted at the garden's rich life.

She loved gardens. Would she have freedom to enjoy its beauty? Inside, people bore expectations. There might be no time for leisure. But once she'd seen the house, Anna knew she belonged here. It was so much like home. She lifted a desperate prayer as they entered the doorway to *Casa de Montaraz*.

Five

Anna's heart pounded as she and Fray Serra followed a male servant across the entry hall. He led them into a large, sunny room in the front of the house. Its side door stood open onto a flagstone patio where a mockingbird perched in the doorway. His golden eye promised a burst into either song or flight. Shafts of light streaked across the polished tiles of the floor.

European furniture, finer than the pieces Porfirio had bartered away, filled the space. She would be surrounded by opulence, if this room was an example.

Fray Serra believed privation to be a protection, but Anna knew she would adapt quite easily to the comforts of *Casa de Montaraz*. The life she was bred to live existed here.

A woman sat before a small fire, legs propped on a footstool. An embroidered silk shawl in rich shades of aqua wrapped her shoulders, and a silver coffee service gleamed beside her. Even on this warm day, a woolen coverlet draped her lap.

Anna's eyes widened as a man arose from a settee

opposite. Surely the most handsome one she had ever seen. His muscular physique filled a short *ranchero's* jacket and slim leather trousers. From a pronounced widow's peak, wavy chestnut hair framed his face. His facial skin had been tanned by exposure to the sun. She was drawn to his eyes, a deep, greenish gray, and then to his mouth. Two dimples bracketed a smile that looked genuine.

Anna smothered a sigh that released inner tensions. She had entertained foolish fears of an employer as wild in appearance as the family name implied. *Montaraz*—untamed. Some *Californios* were rough men, but there was nothing uncultivated in the courtly appearance of Señor de Montaraz. He appeared welcoming. Would his pleasure last after the interview?

At Fray Serra's presentation, Don León de Montaraz bowed over Anna's hand and murmured, "*A sus ordenes*—at your service." Surely not the greeting for a servant, but she was here under the patronage of Fray Serra. He must have stressed her aristocratic lineage. Only a woman of patrician beginnings would do for Don León's wife.

He led her toward the frail woman. "Juliana, my dear, may I present Señorita Anna Arista-Arguello. Of course you recognize our old friend, Fray Serra. Señorita, my wife, Señora Juliana de Montaraz-Silva."

The skin of Juliana's lovely face was unlined, but it stretched over little flesh, with delicate bones visible beneath. Her silvery eyes held an expression of interest. Upon closer examination Anna saw fine lines at their outer corners and something shadowed them for a moment. Pain?

Juliana's frailty made Anna's purpose clear. She

must encourage her to eat healthful foods and lead her into a more active life. She imagined strolls in the lovely garden. She was holding her breath again, waiting for a response. At last, a smile transformed Juliana's face and Anna's heart sang with hope.

"My dear Anna. I shall call you that from the outset and ask that you never burden me with titles. In this male-dominated land I long for female company. Your breeding and intelligence is apparent in your Castilian beauty." She used the formal Spanish reserved for equals.

Anna murmured her thanks in a polite curtsy as Juliana continued. "I want our relationship to be deeper than that of mere usefulness to each other."

"Señora de Montaraz, I am pleased to hear your kind welcome. I will give my best efforts." The words sounded rehearsed. She should have found better.

Don León's head jerked up and he stared at her. Anna had seen the reaction before. The husky voice she inherited from her mother caused surprised reactions, especially in men.

"Juliana," her hostess prompted. "No titles."

Anna hesitated. "I shall be honored." *Mamá wouldn't have allowed such familiarity on sight.*

It couldn't be this simple. Where were the questions? The nerve-shredding interview when she tried to convince herself and her employers that she was suited to service?

Doña Juliana poured and Anna served the coffee, trying to still the tremor in her fingers.

León de Montaraz motioned toward the friar. "Ladies," he said, "seated before you is the man who founded California. Sandal-shod, with only a crucifix to point the way, he came to teach children of the wild. A string of thriving missions is proof of his valor and dedication. In his wake, we *Californios* profit. Without Father Serra's influence, the large ranches of California would not exist."

Don León's speech was scholarly and dramatic, but coming from him, perfect. He sounded a bit like Father.

Fray Serra's lips thinned and he shook his head. "Not the concern of Franciscans, as you well know, Don León. We labor to develop the land first for God and the king of Spain, and then to return it to its original inhabitants when they master agricultural principles. We hold the land in trust for them. Military leaders protect aristocrats' ownership of large tracts, not friars."

The smile did not waver. "Yes, yes, your benign philosophy. All men are brothers. Most commendable, but not very practical on the frontier of civilization. That said, please tell the ladies more of your work among the native peoples."

"The beginning was humble indeed. My fellow friar called California 'this last corner of the earth.' We found a native populace who had no previous contact with Europeans. The *Rumsen* men near Monterey were stoutly built and wore no clothes. I had moments of anxiety concerning their women, but was relieved to find they were decently clothed in skirts made of the leathery leaves of *tules.*"

Don León's eyebrows rose. At the padre's mention of undressed native men, Doña Juliana exchanged a glance with Anna and both smothered smiles. The padre forgot convention when he spoke of purpose.

"They were suspicious of strangers who arrived

in floating houses and rode on unfamiliar animals. The men accepted gifts of beads and clothing but refused offers of food. Foragers and hunters, they ranged forests and fished the sea, but had no metal tools."

Floating houses. Of course. Native people had no experience of large ships and had never seen horses or armored men. Anna had so many questions, but a servant should not inject herself into the conversation.

"After years of labor," the friar continued, "I am rewarded by the devotion of our neophytes. A convert, stone-blind and over eighty years old by his calculations, now conducts the singing. Like many of his people, he has not one gray hair. He pronounces Latin so correctly that I can follow the meaning easily."

Anna glanced toward Doña Juliana. The woman sagged in her chair. "Would a pillow make you more comfortable?"

"Perhaps so."

Señor de Montaraz nodded and smiled as she tucked an embroidered pillow behind his wife. Warmth flooded her. Her employers were gentle people, ready to give her a chance.

After a few more minutes of conversation, Friar Serra arose, insisting he could not remain for the noon meal. "I leave you in good hands, Anna." The old man made the sign of the cross on her forehead and blessed her employers. "*Amar a Dios.* Love God."

It was over. The dreaded interview was finished. She had secured the position. A new life beckoned. "Never look back," Fray Serra had said. But Fray Serra looked back as he neared the door. His eyes met Anna's and her heart constricted. He'd been her lifeline. She didn't want him to leave. He nodded and turned away, apparently satisfied that she was where she belonged.

Don León accompanied the friar out, saying, "I leave you two to become better acquainted."

Doña Juliana was resolute. "No formality between us, Anna." She slipped into informal Spanish. "María will care for my physical needs as she has done for the past two years. Her mother also helps me when her health permits. She's an accomplished needlewoman and María is learning rapidly. From you I want companionship."

That, Anna considered herself able to do. It felt strange to address the older woman informally. It was the language of familiarity, usually reserved for family or friends. After half an hour, she relaxed under Juliana's interest enough to share details of Porfirio's rejection. Her heart warmed at Doña Juliana's indignant expression.

"It's interesting how God works in the affairs of humans," she said. "Had Porfirio been a more dutiful son, a more astute manager, and a much better brother, I wouldn't have you with me. I prayed for a knowledgeable companion who could reduce the encumbrance I am to León."

"I'm sure you represent no encumbrance to your husband."

Juliana shook her head. "He feels compelled to spend hours with me, confined in this house. León is an outdoor man. You'll ease his burden."

"I learn quickly. I want to please you. I'll do whatever you wish, Doña Juliana, although I fear you have acquired a very inexperienced nurse."

"Not a nurse. A companion, Anna. Now dispense with the title once and for all. It makes me feel old.

María will settle you in your room. Then we'll have lunch. The rest of the afternoon is yours. Explore the garden or rest. Tomorrow we'll tour the house."

                                                                  ~

Don León apparently provided well for his servants. María, a girl in her mid-teens, helped Anna settle her few belongings into a large, well-furnished room near the master quarters. It had two windows overlooking the garden and a fireplace with a chair that invited settling in with a book. More than she expected.

That night Anna tossed in the unfamiliar bed. Sleep would not come, despite down pillows and a luxurious satin comforter.

She thought back to the journey along the coastline. To the frightening windstorm and her worries about the character of her employers. Her fears about her inadequacies.

God seemed to have gone before her and smoothed the way, using his agent, Fray Serra. She sighed. Her whole body seemed to deflate, and her mind with it. She had focused on the journey for so long that its culmination was a let-down.

Anna rose to stare out the window and leaned her head against the pane, looking across the courtyard into a night silvered by an invisible moon. She thought of restless nights at home when she had sought comfort looking out at the garden, planning new plantings. The gardeners indulged her, allowing her to dictate the placement of new flower beds.

This was not her garden, but it still worked its magic. She returned to her bed, ready for sleep. She fluffed her pillows and straightened the coverlet.

A strange place, a great distance from everything familiar. Alone among strangers. Even Fray Serra, though near, was inaccessible. Her worst fears come true, yet optimism filled her.

She remembered the friar's analogy about a ship in its harbor out of harm's way. After all her difficult experiences in the past three years, had she found her safe harbor? A fine house, cultured people. What could possibly go wrong?

Six

María knocked on Anna's door the next morning. She led Anna into the enormous kitchens attached to the rear of the house.

"Don León sometimes leaves quite early," she said, "but this morning he stayed to breakfast with Doña Juliana. I served them in their quarters. We have time to eat with the cooks." She pointed to a woman waving at them. "There's Ramona, our head cook."

From behind a table near a windowed wall of the bright and bustling space, a middle-aged woman rose. Apron-wrapped and smiling, she waddled toward them. She spoke before María could make introductions.

"Ramona Saldavar, Anna. News travels fast in this household. Welcome to Rancho de Montaraz." She introduced her flock of kitchen helpers. "Help yourself to the best breakfast in Monterey."

Not an idle boast, Anna decided as she heaped her plate with ham, broiled fish, an egg, and tiny tomatoes as red as rubies. She'd been too excited to eat last evening from the tray sent to her room. María passed a basket of *panecillo* and Anna bit into a small roll, yeasty and crisply-crusted.

"The kitchens are the hub of the ranch, Anna. Unmarried *vaqueros*, freighters and hunters, occasional travelers, even *indios* from the mountains or aristocrats from other ranches—I feed them all." Ramona said.

Much like home, but on a larger scale. Through a large window Anna saw Indian *vaqueros*, the cowboys of the ranch, squatting on their heels, large-roweled spurs beside them. They ate near a window with an outside counter.

Children played *pelota*, managing to keep their leather ball out of harm's way. Others competed for handouts from a large jar of sweets. Spicy cookies and fruit tarts cooled on racks and added mouth-watering aromas to the kitchens. Through an arch she watched cooks in the bakery shove additional pans into wood-fired ovens.

"Heavenly sights and smells, Ramona." Anna rolled her eyes. "I believe your kitchens may become my favorite space."

Ramona smiled. "I'm always prepared for the sweet tooth of Don León. He's partial to fruit tarts, but he never turns down a sugary treat."

There was something at once refreshing and reassuring about Ramona. Her gray hair was wrapped in a careless coil and she cajoled young cooks around her in the voice of experience.

"My grandmother was a girl when Doña Juliana's family was still at Spanish Court," Ramona said. "I follow in my mother's footsteps as *cocinera*, the last in a line of head cooks. I've never married."

Anna saw a sea of shining utensils, stacks of

cooking pots, crates and bags of foodstuffs, wheels of cheeses peeking from cool storage on tiled floors, and a rack filled with a tantalizing array of herbs and spices. Long *ristras,* strings of dried chiles and herbs, hung from support columns and added to the delight of the kitchens' aromas. Ramona's kitchens, however busy they might be, reflected a sense of calm and order, like Ramona herself.

As she took her plate from the table, Ramona called, "Bring another jar of sweets, Anna. You and María can help me serve at the window."

Anna handed out treats to *vaqueros* and children. Her eyes widened as Don León took his place at the end of the line of beggars. The children laughed as he snagged their ball with one hand and hurled it high into the air. Don León swept his hat from his head and bowed low as he reached the window. The children hooted with laughter and danced around him.

"My turn, Señorita," he said with a wicked smile, "and I require a *tartaleta.* No, two."

Anna pushed a curl from her warm forehead with the back of her hand and held out the tarts. "You will need good luck to keep these away from your little friends, Señor."

He took a step nearer and murmured, "Help Ramona keep an eye on that jar. It must never be empty." Grabbing a handful of cookies from a rack, he called over his shoulder, "Until dinner, Señorita. Juliana says you will take your evening meals with us in the *comedor.* Until then."

Anna stammered a good-bye as he strode in the direction of the corrals, munching a tart. He stopped to divide the cookies among several boys at his heels.

"Did I hear him correctly, María? My employers expect me to dine with them? I ate in my room last evening."

"Doña Juliana stressed that you are to take your evening meals in the *comedor*. She considers you a companion. Now I should go to help her dress."

A sweet rush pulsed in Anna's chest. Perhaps she was suited to her task, after all. She must remember to allow Juliana to take the lead. A servant's job was to please.

The rest of her day passed in a flurry of discoveries. The highlight was a tour of the house with Juliana. There was a chapel, where a priest came at intervals to lead services. Anna smothered her disappointment when Juliana made no offer to allow Anna to go to the mission for regular worship and confession. She'd hoped to be able to counsel with Fray Serra often. Perhaps she could bring up the matter later.

They walked in the garden and discussed some of the more unusual plantings. "León plans to rearrange the garden and enlarge it," Juliana said. "He says he'll make the house three times its size." She frowned. "Nothing is ever enough. Except where I'm concerned. My dearest wish goes unanswered."

Anna did not pick up the conversation of discontent. She distracted Juliana with questions and comments and led her to the terrace outside the master quarters. They sipped coffee and Anna read soothing passages from Juliana's prayer book.

Juliana sighed. "Since Fray Serra first mentioned your name, I've anticipated a companion. You exceed my hopes. A woman needs a confidante."

Anna's grip on the book tightened. The thought of

Juliana pouring out her heart was uncomfortable. What could she say? She'd have no wisdom for a married woman ten years her elder. Juliana couldn't mean it. *She's trying to put me at ease about my loss of social status.*

Later Anna chose one of her best dresses for the evening meal. Would there be guests to look askance at a servant dining with them? Mamá had no companion, but Porfirio's tutors didn't dine with the family. It might be tricky to maintain the proper balance since Juliana seemed determined to elevate her companion's status. Señor de Montaraz might have different expectations of a household servant, although he had been the one to mention dinner.

Anna took a deep breath and straightened her posture before she entered the dining room. No guests. Don León and Juliana sat at opposite ends of the table, separated by an expanse of polished wood. Candles, gleaming china, and silver made the table appear ready for a large banquet, instead of three people. A single footman stood ready to serve.

Don León rose and pulled out a chair between them. "Señorita, we welcome you."

Juliana nodded to Anna, but pouting lips replaced her beautiful smile. Dinner progressed without input from the hostess. What was wrong?

Don León seemed oblivious to Juliana's strange behavior. He acted the perfect host, as lively as if he were entertaining a large gathering instead of a servant. When Anna showed interest in ranching, he talked about a recent roundup. Juliana looked on in silence.

"I'm impressed by your knowledge, Anna," Juliana said at last. "The normal pursuits of high-born women do not include interest in ranching operations.

Leó tried to make an outdoor woman of me, but I am not suited to the life."

"A flower whose beauty is best preserved indoors." Don León lifted his glass in salute. Juliana did not acknowledge his smiling toast, and her face settled again into lines of discontent. Don León said no more.

Anna squirmed in her chair, uncertain how to react to the tension between them. Minutes passed. She felt compelled to break the lengthy silence.

"Father was a competent rancher, but his true passion was the sea. He was also drawn to history and read a great deal."

Don León treated her to one of his enchanting smiles. "As do I," he said. "Your father and I may have other interests in common."

Juliana's voice was frosty. "Leó, did you forget Anna's parents are dead? Forgive him, Anna."

Don León colored and nodded. As the meal ended, he remarked, "We are fortunate to find a young lady of good background for Juliana's companion. Perhaps you would enjoy seeing the grant map for Hacienda de Montaraz." He glanced at Juliana, who offered a chilly nod.

"You, as well as I, seem to have found a companion in Anna, León." Juliana rose from the table without excuse and headed for the door. Anna had no wish to lengthen the uncomfortable evening, but duty demanded she follow Juliana to the library where they studied the large map.

Don León had carried his glass of wine with him, finishing the last of several.

"Don't spill on your precious map," Juliana cautioned.

Don León took a deliberate sip, his eyes watching Juliana over the rim of his glass.

Anna looked down at the map. She kept her voice animated. "Amazing. Rancho de Montaraz is twice as large as Father's holding. Fray Serra was instrumental in helping him gain a land grant from the King in the same year listed on your father's map, 1770. They must have been two of the first Californios."

"At present the ranch is the largest in *Alta California*. But I keep an eye out for more land." Pride filled Don León's rich voice. "Our principal sources of revenue are sales of hides and tallow, fresh beef, and the shipment of *carne seca*, the beef we dry on the premises. We ship to Mexico and European ports."

He traced routes on the map. "Quite possibly your father's ships carried our goods. My *caporal*, Antonio Rivera, would know. As foreman he handles much of my business. You must meet him and ask if he knew your father."

Juliana said, "The rest of it, León. Tell Anna what else fills your coffers."

Don León's eyes narrowed in her direction. "I profit from sales of horses to soldiers, fur trappers, traders, and an occasional traveler, and I am training some of my Indian laborers to trade with other tribes for furs—sea otter, seal, and beaver. I am also in the process of establishing a hemp plantation. It takes many sources of revenue to provide for the large number of employees the ranch requires."

"Admit the truth, León. He is never content, Anna, unless he is making money. Our aristocratic ancestors would sniff in disapproval at the taint of his mercenary interests. He sells even the skins of bears and deer killed by his hunters."

Don León stared at his wife. Strong color rose in his face, but he did not reply. Anna struggled to keep her shock from showing.

"Father believed in enterprise—" she began, but Juliana's expression stopped her. She lowered her eyes to the map during an uneasy silence. Don León finished his wine and excused himself, saying he had work to complete in his office.

Anna was at a loss. Juliana would be accustomed to speaking frankly in the company of servants, but she had been rude in Anna's presence. Don León's embarrassment seemed to mean nothing to her.

Tossed back into conflict. Her stomach rolled. How hard would it be to maintain neutrality?

Anna pled a headache and left Juliana. She hurried to her quarters, replaying the events of the evening. Later, she knelt and offered a lengthy prayer for Don León and Doña Juliana.

A particular scent drew Anna into the kitchen early the next morning. Ramona toasted cacao beans on a griddle until they popped like corn. The aroma was indescribable.

"Only I can properly judge the beans' readiness," Ramona said. "After they're toasted to perfection, I grind them, along with brown sugar, vanilla beans, and cinnamon bark, to form a paste."

Anna watched her smooth the dark concoction into round wooden molds. "Fit for King Carlos, Ramona."

Ramona shaved off a chunk of the crunchy paste. Dropping it into a glazed pitcher, she took up a carved *molinillo*. Its pestle bottom softened and ground the chocolate while Anna poured heated milk into the vessel.

When Ramona spun the grooved pestle between her palms, it created a rich froth. With brisk whirling, the liquid became a heady elixir of dark chocolate, sensuously perfumed by cinnamon. A mist of tan foam tickled Anna's lips.

"A little bit of heaven, Ramona."

The two women sat on stools to one side of the kitchen, out of the way of busy cooks. They talked of household news, which Ramona delivered with compassion and humor. They laughed several times and Anna decided she could rely on Ramona's gentle wisdom. As she spoke of Porfirio's abandonment, Ramona reached for her hand.

Anna managed a smile. "All in the past, Ramona. I wanted you to know the truth. But now I need ideas about Doña Juliana's diet. She should gain some weight."

"It's not the food, Anna. I know what she likes. I believe she'll eat more now that you're with her. She sometimes sends lunch trays back untouched, but perhaps you can encourage her."

"We'll celebrate each empty plate," Anna promised.

Could she question Ramona about her employers? What was at the root of Juliana's coldness last evening? Servants had ears even though they went unacknowledged by their aristocratic employers. Ramona was clearly the mistress among servants, but it would be inappropriate to ask. Perhaps the unpleasant atmosphere would not be repeated.

Seven

A week had gone by. The garden was beautiful in late June. Birds filled the trees, ready for a night's rest. Anna strolled with her employers after a relaxing dinner, during which Juliana smiled and laughed.

Don León looked down at his wife. "I want you to plan a woman's garden. I have sources to find any plant in the world. We'll make it exactly what you want it to be."

"Do you mean that, Leó? You won't take it over and make it grandiose?"

"It will be your garden. As big or as small as you decide." He smiled. "In the spring when I begin enlarging the house, we'll create it. And Anna might help you."

"She loves gardens. It will be a worthy project— don't you agree, Anna?"

"Oh, yes, Juliana. I'll enjoy helping you."

Keeping the peace with her was a bit like walking on egg shells, but she'd won Anna's heart. It was obvious why Don León loved his wife. She was beautiful and intelligent. More than a bit self-centered but charming.

"We met Antonio Rivera in the garden today on his way to your office," Juliana said. "He said he knew Anna's father. Tell her about Antonio, Leó."

"The best *caporal* in the countryside. He manages ranch affairs for me. We were boyhood friends and he sometimes shared my schooling. His father came from Spain with mine and married an Indian woman in Mexico. A man of integrity. You can trust Antonio in any matter."

Perhaps a man worth knowing. "I hope to see him again and ask for his memories of Father." Their brief encounter had left Anna with an image of a man with charm of his own. He appeared a few years older than Don León.

Don León said, "Antonio also trains my riding stallions. No finer horseman in California."

Juliana added, "His wife and three children died some years ago in an epidemic of *cuello negro,* the black throat that native people die of every year. Soldiers brought the disease to California."

She crossed herself at the very mention of the feared respiratory infection that caused a tough, fibrous coating to cover the throat and sometimes blocked airways.

Anna shuddered. "How sad."

"It was," Don León said. "Antonio treasured his wife and family. I think he grieves to this day."

I like him already. Maybe I'll see him soon.

As if in answer to her wish, the next morning Antonio Rivera sat with her and Ramona at breakfast.

Anna found herself drawn to his calm voice and good-natured expression. The large hand stirring his coffee was clean with well-trimmed nails, and he looked immaculate in his work clothes. A ready smile and soft, chocolate-brown eyes softened rugged features. *A man at peace with himself.*

"You said yesterday that you knew my father, Rodrigo Arista. Did you do business with him?"

Antonio nodded. "His ships carried hides and beef for us and brought goods from other ports in New Spain. An honest man. I know you miss him."

"So much." She swallowed the rising lump.

Ramona came to her rescue with a question for Antonio, and Anna was soon able to join the conversation again as they spoke of ranching affairs. It was clear that Antonio admired Don León. And that he had a strong faith in God. References to both were sprinkled liberally in his speech.

"My life is invested in this land," he said. "And I count myself fortunate to have a friend as employer." He smiled at Anna. "You've come to a good place. Call on me for anything, Señorita. Ramona can send a kitchen boy to find me anywhere on the ranch. I usually tell her which range I'll be working."

"A true friend," Ramona said. "When hard times arise, some so-called friends fall away." She and Antonio exchanged a look that spoke of shared experiences.

Porfirio and Pedro. Two men who should have stood by her. It still hurt more than Anna cared to admit. "I, too, know something of fair-weather friends." Her voice sounded a bit wobbly and she wished she hadn't spoken. It was time to move on.

Antonio's sympathetic brown gaze found hers.

"Any time, Señorita, if I can help."

Languid days of late summer gave way to the approach of fall. Juliana's moodiness surfaced regularly and didn't appear to be related to her health. On the days when Anna could persuade her, they ventured out to the garden, and occasionally, in a small open carriage, as far as the Carmel River, a quarter mile from the house.

One late August afternoon they found a secluded cove perfect for swimming. With Juliana acting as her laughing sentinel, Anna swam in her chemise.

Out of the blue, that evening at dinner Don León said, "Señorita, do you enjoy swimming?"

She glanced up at him, color rising in her cheeks, and he laughed. "Not to worry. Antonio and I were atop the ridge and you were submerged. I have been enticed by the beauty of that cove myself."

Juliana laughed with him. "León keeps an eye on everything. He is in control, without question. Come with us to the sitting room after dinner, Anna. I told him of your schooling in Mexico City and asked him to show you his books. They're his most treasured possessions. If the house burned, he would save them first and then me."

"Now, Juli," he chided. "My wife says she enjoys your reading to her. Perhaps you will read for us tonight, Señorita."

Anna turned to Juliana. "Will you choose a selection?"

She chose a rather gloomy poem that Anna had read to her on several occasions. Its theme was the disappointment of unrealized dreams.

Don León smiled. "You read well, Señorita, despite it being a difficult passage I could not understand."

Juliana's face hardened. "Of course not. None of your aspirations are denied. Only mine."

Anna's heart sank, but Don León didn't react, and Juliana's voice brightened. "You must show her your book collection, León. She can appreciate your continuing quest for knowledge."

Don León arose and invited Anna to come to one of the shelves lining the sitting room. The books, filling shelf after shelf, reminded her of Father's collection. She loved books. Don León pointed out volumes on many subjects, including the sciences.

"One must never stop learning, Señorita. Take any of the books that appeal to you. I'll be delighted to discuss any topic you wish."

"He will," Juliana offered. "He's forever willing to discuss his books. I sometimes take refuge in my needle work while he expounds." Her voice grew sharp. "In other matters he's not so forthcoming."

Juliana's comments sound critical. What does she find unsatisfactory in her courtly, attentive husband?

Don León shrugged and smiled at Anna's choice of a gardening book. "Perhaps she'll find some ideas for your woman's garden, Juliana. I'll make it perfect for you."

Anna took a short turn through the front garden on her way back from the kitchen to Juliana's suite. Time to think. Ideas for Juliana's garden might come to her. Mid-September—she'd been at Hacienda de

Montaraz for three months. Visitors were frequent and life was interesting.

Juliana's unpredictable personality, for the most part, was not a problem. On bad days it was María who suffered. On good days Juliana laughed and talked, but even then sometimes withdrew into silence, her expression dissatisfied. What disturbed her?

Don León made up for Juliana's moodiness. He entertained each evening with charming stories of the day's happenings or tales of history. But something was amiss between her employers. What reason could Juliana possibly have to be unhappy? Her husband was handsome and attentive. She lived in a fine house and lacked for nothing.

Anna wanted to warn her not to take for granted her easy life. "Enjoy your abundance," she wanted to say. "It could disappear." Hardly words for a servant.

She shook her head. "Not my problem. I'm out to enjoy the garden." She'd spoken aloud and peered around, but no gardener was in sight.

Under an oak, a few crunchy acorns lay scattered among the leaf litter that padded the path. Anna looked back at the house. Its warm brown walls and red tiled roof merged into a blaze of surrounding trees, making it look like a painting.

A slanting morning sun on red Catalina brush cherries near the path caught her eye, and then the brilliance of a blue jay. The sycamore's rusty leaves fluttered and tossed in a sudden breeze.

"Music in them." Anna caught one as it fell and twirled around in a carefree dance, stopping only when she was out of breath.

"Supposed to bring a day of good luck. Nonsense,

of course. Luck does not shape the life of a follower of God. It is His Holy Spirit who—"

"A worthy thought, Anna."

She whirled as Don León's warm voice startled her. How long had he been watching? "You are not the first to catch me thinking aloud, Don León."

Hat in hand, he smiled down at her embarrassment. His polished boots gleamed. His form-fitting vest contrasted with the full sleeves of his immaculate linen shirt and emphasized the width of his shoulders.

She looked away.

He gestured toward the house and she caught a masculine scent of soap and body-warmed leather. Anna took a step back.

"Juliana saw you from the breakfast table window and sent me. She says you enjoy riding. Would you like to choose a mount this morning?"

Anna hesitated. They couldn't ride without a *chaperona*. Another woman must accompany them.

"You may enjoy exploring more of the ranch. We both want you to enjoy some leisure. You work hard and have accomplished wonders in Juliana's life. Her health improves under your care and she has a new interest in living."

For a moment Anna was lost in Don León's astonishing eyes. They were the color of moss this morning.

"I'll be honored to accompany you at times, Señorita, as will Antonio. But you must have a horse. You can use my wife's saddle. Juliana has never embraced riding. Of course, a female can attend us."

"I do enjoy it," Anna admitted. *Nothing wrong with time off if it is offered.* "Father taught me to ride as soon as I was able to stay in a saddle. Even my mother enjoyed the sport."

"Then we'll go to the stables at once. My horses are my pride. The bloodlines have been in my family for generations. I have several candidates in mind, but you must make the final choice." He kicked at a toadstool peeking from its leafy lair on the littered path. "I must remind the gardeners to rake the pathways."

Anna hid a smile. Nothing escaped his quest for perfection.

They strolled to the barn, entering a walled barnyard through its substantial gateway. A bronze shield emblazoned with a stylized *M*, the cattle brand of Rancho de Montaraz, topped the gateway. The barn itself was a two-story red adobe. Adjoining the impressive barn were stables and a corral with strips of rawhide lashing its posts.

"The barn is an unusual color."

Don León said, "It was the first building finished on the hacienda. My father built it quickly as a temporary family residence. The color is one he saw in the Yucatán, reputed to bring good fortune. Like catching a falling leaf, I suppose. Foolishness to a bright young woman."

Anna laughed. Don León's stories about family traditions reminded her of Father's. The two would have found much in common.

He sent an *establero* to summon a servant girl to ride with them. Anna was soon mounted in a small side saddle on a dark bay Galiceno named Consuelo. She stroked the mare's neck. "Consuelo is a beauty. A well-proportioned head and straight profile."

"A fine choice, Señorita. Not too large but intelligent and well-trained. A spirited mount for a spirited woman."

She nibbled on her bottom lip. He shouldn't make such a personal comment. A glance showed Don León wasn't looking at her and she relaxed. He put his black Andalusian through several complicated maneuvers—a work of art astride the stallion. The animal was quick in response to movements of his rider's muscular thighs.

His thighs? Mamá would faint. What is wrong with me? Anna looked away, her mind racing. This had to stop.

He reined up at her side and Anna squirmed under his intense gaze. Had her inappropriate thoughts showed on her face? She searched for a comment. "Father said a rider and a well-trained mount are a song. A harmony of rhythm and movement." She sounded inane, but Don León nodded.

"Emphasis is always on the quality of the horse rather than how quickly the goal is reached."

Anna smothered a sigh of relief. She needn't worry. Don León was forever the gentleman. But never again would she indulge in such unseemly attention toward him.

Eight

Anna looked back to check on Elodia. The young servant girl struggled to keep her horse to the pace set by Don León. "Come on, Elodia. I'll wait for you."

Don León returned to where Anna and Elodia rested their horses. He handed a water flask to the servant and said, "Stay for a while under the trees. Señorita Anna and I will be a little farther up the trail."

Elodia dismounted and limped toward a large rock. She sat gingerly, then stood and leaned against it.

"Poor Elodia. She has probably never ridden before. I'm glad you allowed her to rest."

"It's not far, but she looks like she is in pain." Don León smiled at Anna. "Not many women can ride as well as you."

He and Anna rode another quarter mile and dismounted, still within sight of Elodia. He pointed to a large boulder.

"The eastern edge. I've shown you each of the four boundary stones marking the borders of Rancho de Montaraz." Don León held out his arms as if to embrace his surroundings. "The land has its limits, but not my vision for it. It will be my legacy to the Californias. An example of what can be done."

Anna looked out over the vast space that stretched away to the mountains. She murmured something, but her mind wandered. Don León's expectations were grandiose, but so were his capabilities. He would build the empire of his dreams, but why? What drove him?

He had no children to inherit the fruit of his labors. He needed a son—perhaps several. Men to cherish the land as he did and continue the proud name of de Montaraz.

Anna's next riding companion was Antonio. With Elodia always behind them, they rode to the mouth of a canyon, where a waterfall splashed diamonds into the pool beneath.

"The landscape of the ranch has some lovely surprises, Antonio."

"There are many more. I look forward to showing them to you. You seem to have a feel for the land."

"Let's dismount, Antonio, and give Elodia a rest. She looks exhausted."

But the next morning, three hours before Juliana was usually up, Elodia was at the corrales with Anna and Don León. She stood with them for a few minutes, then yawned and walked stiffly toward the shelter of the barn.

"Elodia is miserable, Don León. Would it be proper to excuse her as my riding companion?"

"Are you comfortable riding alone with me?"

Anna paused and then said, "I am, Don León, if

Juliana approves."

They turned their attention to the two men training young stallions. One was Antonio and the other a young vaquero. In the male-dominated culture of a hacienda, it was beneath the dignity of a vaquero to ride anything other than a stallion.

"This one is almost ready." Don León mused. "Watch how the animal obeys the nudge of a knee or the imperceptible tug of the bit in his mouth."

"Antonio's patience and expertise are remarkable. You and he must be among the best horsemen in the countryside."

"Thank you, Señorita. It's rewarding to share the experience with someone who appreciates it." Don León flashed his enchanting smile.

Anna turned her gaze back to Antonio. A colorful bandana wrapped his forehead, and his hair was braided beneath the flat-brimmed hat. Traditional dress for a charro, when he trained horses.

After half an hour, Antonio dismounted and strode over to the corral fence. "Good animal, Don León." He pushed back his hat and removed his bandana. His warm brown eyes sought Anna's. "What did you think, Señorita?"

Anna smiled. "You're born to the saddle, Antonio. One with your horse, as my father said of natural horsemen."

Antonio laughed. "A true compliment from an accomplished rider like yourself. I've thought of another place to take you on our next ride. This ranch has some beautiful spots."

"I look forward to another lovely sight." She smiled at him and glanced toward Don León. He'd said nothing about the training session. His expression caused her to draw a sharp breath.

Don León stared from one to the other, his face stiff and disapproving. He crooked his arm.

"We must return to the house, Señorita. Juliana is, no doubt, ready for your companionship."

Anna didn't answer Antonio's good-bye. Don León looked irritated as he marched her toward the house. Was he worried they had left Juliana too long, or was he upset by the familiarity that had developed between her and Antonio?

She liked being with Antonio. She felt safe, at peace in her soul in his company. He even prayed with her at times. But she never tried to keep him from his duties. There was no need for Don León to be disturbed.

She panted as she trotted to keep up with his furious pace. Elodia puffed along behind them. Half way to the house Anna had enough. She stopped and disengaged her arm.

"There is no need for you to accompany me further, Don León. I will go at once to Doña Juliana." Her voice sounded sharper than she intended, but even a servant had some say over her actions.

Don León looked at her. A line appeared between his brows and then his face set in lines of displeasure. He bowed a stiff farewell before he turned away and marched toward the corrals.

Anna drew her bottom lip between her teeth, watching him stalk away. She hadn't handled the situation well, but Don León's attitude was puzzling. Did he imagine impropriety on Antonio's part when they were together, or that Anna might neglect her job to seek his company? Antonio was Anna's friend as he was Ramona's friend. Why should their relationship matter to Don León?

Fall slid into cooler, rainy days of winter, and Anna was grateful for the fireplaces that blazed throughout the house. Juliana's winter parlor boasted two kivas, the beehive fireplaces of Indian origin.

Fires crackled in both on this November day, filling the room with drowsy warmth. Juliana's needlework pillows lining the bancos on either side of the fireplace invited Anna to sit and toast her toes. But first she must see to Juliana's comfort.

She drew the top curtain of the large window, regretting even the partial loss of light seeping through the leaden overcast. The sky was hung in various shades of slate, while mists shrouded distant peaks. Frequent showers of raindrops the size of coins pelted the glass.

"Is the chimney drawing properly?" Juliana drew her shawl closer and said, "I've been cold all morning."

Anna added another log to both fireplaces. She tugged heavy wrought iron screens back into place. If she stayed busy, she might keep her thoughts from how much she missed sunny autumn days when she rode beside Antonio or Don León.

She smiled at Juliana, but received only a wan response. She looked tired this morning, aged by the web of lines at the corners of her eyes. The embroidery needle in her slender hands poked in and out without its usual rhythm. She laid the needlework in her lap and stared at up Anna.

"I want children. I must give León a son and heir, but he will not allow me another pregnancy in my

present health. We lost two. I want a baby—any baby."
Her lip curled and her voice became bitter. "León refuses
the idea of adoption. He says a baby would be more
than I could manage. He sees me as a weak woman."
She covered her face with her hands. "He doesn't even
want me to visit the graves of our daughters. Says it
only upsets me."

Anna's heart seemed to freeze. Juliana's
discontent was suddenly clear, but so was Don León's
concern. She went to her knees and took Juliana's hand.

"I'll soon be too old for motherhood, Anna. I'm
four years older than León. I would rather die trying to
give birth than to live a childless life."

What could she say? Anna drew Juliana into her
arms as she would a child. "You're cold." She brought
another fringed Spanish shawl to add to the one already
wrapping the frail shoulders.

Juliana shivered again, her eyes focused on the
abandoned needlework. Anna added a blanket to wrap
her legs.

"Something hot to drink, Juliana?"

Tears shimmered in her eyes. "I'm sorry. I can't
believe I blurted out my troubles. I should never burden
you, a young unmarried woman, with intimacies of my
troubled marriage, but you've become a friend over
these past months. Please forgive me and try to forget I
ever spoke of this. León must not know."

Within a few minutes Don León came in and
brought with him the fresh scent of outdoors. Drops of
moisture in his hair sparkled as he bent to kiss Juliana's
cheek before he removed his black woolen cloak.
Anna glimpsed a scarlet satin lining and admired the
ceremony he made of hanging it on an arm of the coat

tree opposite his sword and silver spurs.

He smiled at her. "You've made this a cozy space with its two fires. Will you ladies allow me to join you for coffee? All morning rain clouds seemed pressed against the top of my hat and I'm chilled to the bone. I can use some of Ramona's hot chocolate or coffee and one of her good apple tartaletas."

Anna returned from the kitchen with a tray holding a pot of coffee and one of rich chocolate, along with a plate of Ramona's still-warm apple tartlets. She was thrilled to see Juliana smiling and watched her finish an entire mug of chocolate and most of a tart in her husband's company.

Don León spoke with an easy grace, telling a story of an orphan calf he'd brought to the barnyard. Both women laughed at the comical ending.

"If I may say so, Señorita, I've always thought your laugh is as surprising as your somewhat husky voice."

Anna's color heightened under his tender smile. Juliana looked from one to the other and Anna's stomach knotted. Much to Anna's relief, Juliana smiled.

"You've become like one of the family, Anna. León is thankful I have you. He can spend more time with his beloved animals."

Anna cleared away the dishes and retired to her apartment, eager to get away before the acrimony began in earnest. She stared out the window, thinking of Juliana's revelation. Sympathy weighted her chest. Both were to be pitied. Don León must want a child as much as Juliana did, but not if it meant losing his wife. A devastating choice.

But adoption should be a safe alternative. She

and María could look after the baby, and Don León could hire an experienced wet nurse. On the other hand, Juliana was a worrier. She would obsess about the baby's every upset. Fray Serra said at the outset that her mental health was precarious. Don León must feel he couldn't risk it.

Ironic. Wealth could not guarantee happiness. Healthy children played in the courtyard every day, seeming to come along whether they were planned or not, and two loving people who could offer a good life were left wanting.

Anna dropped to her knees. "Holy Father of mercy, please take this into Your hands. If it is not right for Juliana to bear children, please soften Don León's attitude toward adoption. At the mission there must be many orphans. He could offer a fine life to one Your little ones."

Even before the celebration of La Navidad, Anna longed for spring. The Christmas season had been dear to her. She'd loved the celebrations and solemn holy days of her youth. This year would be different, but it had to be better than the three sad Christmases after her parents' deaths. She was often alone while Porfirio celebrated somewhere without her. Juliana said Hacienda de Montaraz would host several festivities of the season.

On clear winter days Anna sometimes convinced Juliana to bundle up and venture out to watch gardeners clearing borders, cutting sodden stalks, and digging bulbs and dormant plants to be relocated. The work on the house was planned to begin in spring.

When gray days trapped the women inside, they decorated in anticipation of coming feast days. Antonio brought bundles of cypress and pine boughs. Bedrooms were readied in anticipation of guests and received their share of decorations.

"Thank goodness your patience is limitless, Antonio," Anna said one morning in early December. "Juliana said that swag must be moved several inches higher."

He grinned and did as he was asked. "There cannot be much work left in this room," he said, hands on his hips, surveying the entry hall. "Every surface is decorated."

Fall apples joined bitter Spanish oranges and lemons in arrangements and evergreens on the fireplace mantel, stair rails, windowsills, table tops, and chandeliers.

"Probably not enough for Juliana. She'll find other spots. Wait and see."

Antonio's laugh was good natured. "Well, I don't mind. When I'm working in the house, there is your company and Ramona's hot chocolate. Both are very fine."

The next morning before Juliana came down, Don León found Anna arranging a display on the mantel of the morning room. "Juliana says you two make a fine team. You have an eye for beauty."

Anna busied her hands with the greens, trying to ignore the blood she felt warming her ears. Why was she so shy at his compliment? "Thank you, Don León."

"My wife's precarious health makes visits to other ranches impossible, but that won't limit the number of visitors. I'm pleased that you help her enjoy the preparations. You enrich life on the ranch for us all."

"The season reminds me of home," she said.

He bent to sniff at fragrant greens surrounding a substantial candle on a tabletop. His gaze caught hers. "This is your home. You must never leave us, Anna."

Her fingers trembled among the greens. "I am happy here," she said. What she felt went far beyond happiness. Nothing could make her leave the safe haven she had found.

Later, she found Juliana giving instructions to María about altering two ball gowns spread out on her bed.

"We want these to be the latest fashion, Anna. They are yours."

Tears rose in Anna's eyes. "So generous of you."

"Put on the blue one and let María mark the lines to fit you."

Anna slipped into the dress and studied her reflection in the mirror. María fussed around her, planning alterations to the beautiful gown. Its rich blue silk shimmered with tiny seed pearls.

Anna tugged upward on the fitted bodice. "Is it cut too low?"

Juliana laughed. "Just low enough. Young gallants will be smitten."

Perhaps. Until they discover I'm a servant. But Juliana's gift warmed her. If only she were as generous and kind to Don León.

Holy Days dawned on December sixteenth. Families began disembarking from carriages and liveried footmen hastened to care for blooded animals that rivaled one another in spirit and beauty. Noble horses constituted the pride of any Spanish hacienda.

Anna watched visitors revel in the hospitality

of Rancho de Montaraz, renewing acquaintances and exchanging news. Isolation of far-flung ranches required that some remain for days. The house rang with laughter of adults and children.

Don León said, "Anna, you must join us at the ball this evening. I look forward to dancing with you."

Juliana said, "Wear the blue dress. You'll outshine even me."

Before the party in the great ballroom, Anna joined the servants' festivities in the kitchen courtyard. She and Ramona clapped along with others while guitars strummed and dancers whirled and bobbed in staccato rhythms. Men lit holgueras, traditional bonfires, and jumped over them, as watchers chanted prayers for protection against disease.

Later, she joined her employers in the ballroom. Juliana appeared revitalized in her element as charming hostess, a gracious and smiling Don León at her side. No one would guess at the private tension between them.

The Governor of Monterey was present. His gaze roved the ballroom while his magpie wife filled the air with chatter. Ramona said he had a woman stashed away for relief. Anna's heart went out to the talkative little woman as she stood beside her, pretending to listen to the endless words. She was soon rescued by Don León.

Of the many partners Anna had at the ball, he was the most accomplished dancer. His conversation sparkled with compliments as they danced.

"I notice young hotspurs vying for your attention. Do not trust any of them, Señorita. Not one of them is worthy of you."

Worthy or not, none of them would seek a serious alliance with her. The sons of aristocrats would gladly entertain a dalliance with her, but they would look to Spain or Mexico for wives if a woman of wealth was not available in California.

Later, her gaze followed him as he danced with an elderly woman. She remarked to Juliana, "None of the caballeros compare to Don León. He dances with a grace beyond any of them and he's attentive to all the guests, young and old."

Juliana raised an eyebrow. "León has always had a string of admirers, but I had the most impeccable lineage and the largest dowry."

Nine

On a bright January day, Anna watched Don León
enter Juliana's sitting room, hat in hand. "My dear,
what do you think of Anna riding with me to see last
night's snowfall in the high country? Unfortunately,
Elodia is with her sick mother. Is it appropriate for
Anna to ride without a *chaperona*?"

Anna wanted to dance on her toes. Snow was
a rarity in Alta California. A chance to ride in snow-
covered mountains might never happen again.

"Look at her." Juliana smiled. "Eagerness
personified. I see nothing wrong with you and Anna
riding unaccompanied if she's comfortable with the
idea of miserable cold. Bundle up, Anna. León will not
know when to call a halt."

"Her way with words will make you feel as if you
witnessed it yourself." Don León bent to kiss Juliana's
cheek.

"The only way I could enjoy it. Off with you two
adventurers. Send María to me as you go."

Anna's fingers fumbled as she dressed in her

riding clothes. Brightly wrapped against the cold by a scarlet scarf encircling her head and neck, she tightened her hat string and followed Don León to the corrals.

He saddled Consuelo, his every movement deft and experienced. Did he ever falter?

"Pull on your gloves before you mount, Señorita. You'll need them where we're going."

The two riders moved side by side, suspended in time, drawn by the vision of white grandeur above. The mare pranced in excitement in the frigid air as the slope increased. Windblown fantasies disguised ordinary features and built fairy castles, and a hush cloaked the forest.

"When I see the mountains like this, I wish I could live here as the bears do, wild and content." Don León turned to Anna, his eyes sparkling. "How would I look in fur?"

She laughed with him. "Personally, Don León, I would miss crackling fires and occasional mugs of hot chocolate."

His gaze softened and lingered on hers. She thought he was about to say more, but he turned back to the trail. They rode for another hour in the fantasy world, exchanging only occasional comments.

An animal barked, the sound sharp and unexpected in the silence. Consuelo's eyes flared and she whinnied, but Don León's firm hand was on her halter before she could rear.

"Keep a tight rein, Señorita. That was a gray fox. Many other animals up here. Bears will be deep into hibernation now." He pointed to a high ridge. "Mule deer reside there in numbers, as do their predators, mountain lions."

Anna shivered and Don León reached out a gloved hand to tuck the scarf tighter around her neck. He leaned near and in the cold light she could see herself reflected in his remarkable eyes. She couldn't look away. His fingers tightened on her shoulder and he whispered, "You're in no danger, Anna. I will keep you safe."

Consuelo took a step forward and the spell broke. Anna sucked in a deep breath of frigid air and coughed. The don's snowy handkerchief appeared and she used it to cover her confusion. To her relief, Don León spoke of ordinary things as they prodded the horses forward; but her thoughts were still on what had happened between them.

His touch and the sound her name on his lips were unsettling, but not as much as what she thought she'd read in his eyes. Most troubling of all was the way her heartbeat quickened in response.

What was wrong with her? She was being foolish. Don León was only being protective, just as he was with Juliana. He thought of her as family.

"On tall peaks," she heard him say, "winter shows her face for a while. Shallow mountain lakes freeze, and the gardeners cut ice for our cellar, so we benefit, along with the river, from snow in the mountains. Spring is lovely up here, Señorita, but nothing rivals the magnificence of a fresh snowfall. Your loveliness furnishes the final adornment."

Her stomach fluttered but she managed to meet his eyes. "I appreciate the opportunity to see all this and recreate the splendor for Doña Juliana. I only wish her health permitted her a more adventurous life."

"I wish that as well, but she is like the many

women who do not enjoy the outdoor life. I've never known one quite like you."

She didn't know what to say. He cut a striking figure astride his black stallion. His black woolen cape showed a hint of its scarlet lining in the center of his broad chest. He was far too attractive and his compliments felt too good. She enjoyed being admired by a handsome man—any woman would. But this one was Juliana's husband. She had no right to be assessing his physical magnetism.

A retreat was in order. They were alone up here. She manufactured a shiver. "Perhaps we should return. I'm beginning to feel uncomfortable." And not just from the cold, she added to herself.

"I have a flask of warmed wine. Would that help? I'm reluctant for our adventure to end." He moved the Andalusian nearer until their stirrups touched. "Will you accept my cloak?" His hands moved to unfasten its closure.

She could not allow it. However much she would have enjoyed the comfort of his body-warmed garment, she must put a stop to it. "I am ready to return, Don León."

"As you wish, Señorita. I would not want you to take a chill."

When Anna arrived in the morning room, Juliana listened, smiling at the enthusiastic word pictures Anna painted.

"All you left out were frost-bitten fingers and red, running noses," she said. "I went with León once. Once was enough."

Juliana's gay mood continued throughout the day. The women never seemed to lack for topics of interest. To Anna's relief she had not spoken of a baby since the holidays.

That night Anna looked out frost-rimmed windows into the garden, silvered in the light of a winter moon. Even at lower levels a dusting of snow had fallen, loving every tree, shrub, and stone it touched with its crystalline majesty.

A rare occurrence, he says. I shall never forget this day—but it should have been Juliana beside him.

An artist from México City arrived two weeks later to paint portraits of the couple. Many fine days were now interspersed amid rainy ones.

While Juliana sat for her portrait, Don León and Anna often rode. His talk was always of improvements and innovations he planned for the hacienda.

"I've employed stoneworkers to build an *acequia* to bring river water to the house," he said one day. "The wells are inadequate for new plantings I intend to introduce." His eyes shone.

If only his interest in adopting a child matched his plans for his wife's surroundings. Melancholy spells had returned to torment Juliana. She'd said to Anna, "I insisted upon including a nursery suite in the renovations, and León agreed, but he still refuses to speak of adoption." The thought of empty rooms made Anna's throat ache.

Juliana began complaining of chest pain that kept her awake and one morning demanded that Don León send to the mission for a doctor.

"You know I mistrust *medicos* and their concoctions. What you need, Juliana, is fresh air and activity. Look at the bloom on Anna's cheeks. She benefits from the outdoors. Enjoy it with her."

Moments later Don León's shoulders slumped under Juliana's attack and he finally nodded. "As you wish. I'll send for a doctor."

Anna felt like crying. He was right. How could Juliana be so cruel?

Dr. Sanchez arrived with a young Indian nurse. His youth and nervous manner were not lost on Anna. He didn't look much older than she was. Could he really relieve a condition that had plagued Juliana for years?

Juliana explained her problem at length. Dr. Sanchez nodded toward the nurse, who opened a small valise she carried. The doctor rummaged inside and withdrew a single unpolished glove. At the doctor's request the nurse helped Juliana to lie flat on a long bench at the foot of the bed.

Don León stood stiffly by and glowered. The doctor knelt beside Juliana as the nurse placed his bag on the floor beside him. Casting a nervous glance up at Don León, he said, "I will need to use direct percussion on your wife's...*uh*, chest." He drew on the leather glove. "I must tap the region of her heart."

Don León scowled. "And what will you learn from that?"

"I can determine whether there is fluid in the lungs."

"Let him get on with his examination," Juliana snapped. "I'm uncomfortable on this bench." She adjusted her dress. "Hold my hand, Anna."

Dr. Sanchez struck Juliana's chest with the points of two extended fingers and bent his head to listen. She winced and squeezed Anna's fingers. After three taps, he rose to his feet. Don León helped Juliana sit up.

"Well?" His voice was impatient.

Dr. Sanchez cleared his throat and removed the glove. "No sign of congestion. The tension in her neck and the headaches she describes make me think your wife's problem is a nervous disorder. This should help." He withdrew a fair-sized corked bottle from the case. "A tincture of opium and camphor, widely used in Europe, but only recently available in the Californias."

Don León frowned. "How will it help her? It must not cause her to sleep during the daytime. She does too much of that already."

The doctor's hand holding the bottle began to shake until Juliana took it from him. "León, I insist on trying the new medicine. I won't take it during the day. Anything to relieve my pain and allow me to sleep at night."

Don León glared at the doctor. "Follow me to my office. You must write out a dosage schedule, and I'll pay you for your services."

Anna's prayers were rewarded when the next morning Juliana awoke after a night of unbroken rest. A single dose had worked a miracle, but within three days her appetite vanished and she complained of pain again. Anna fussed around her, trying to relieve her discontent, but she had returned to the old refrain.

"It's his fault, Anna. We could have a beautiful son and heir if León were not so stubborn about adoption. If I had a child, I wouldn't need medication. I'd be happy."

Anne bit back an answer. It seemed unfair of Juliana to blame her husband. Perhaps he was overprotective, but she'd become unreasonable. A loving husband didn't deserve such treatment. She must distract Juliana from her destructive thoughts.

Anna's enthusiasm pulled Juliana back outdoors to plan the garden. They staked out flower beds and marked locations for shrubs and pathways. If she could help Juliana embrace Don León's dream, perhaps he would become more open to hers.

Anna felt a thrill of encouragement when Don León joined them on the second afternoon. After a time he said, "We need to tell Anna what we discussed last night."

"We want your input on an apartment for yourself, Anna. We'll adjoin it to the nursery." Juliana gave Don León a steady look. He nodded.

"And you'll have a study, perhaps with a door onto the balcony. Does that sound acceptable?" Don León's smile was tender.

Anna couldn't speak. Tears rose in her eyes.

"You'll always have a home with us," he said, "and we want it to suit your taste."

As she returned to her room, Fray Serra's words echoed in her mind. *A safe harbor*. She'd come to Casa de Montaraz fearing uncharted seas. Instead she had anchored among good people and could look forward to a future on the ranch. Overcome, Anna retreated to her room and knelt in a prayer of thanksgiving.

The one rocky reef that jutted into her tranquil cove was Juliana's discontent. If only she would become more understanding of her husband, everything would be perfect.

Ten

In late February the air was filled with the promise of spring. Anna finished a walk in the garden and a prayer for Don León and Juliana, two forever on her mind. She returned to the dining room to find them still poring over plans for the house and gardens.

Juliana's face and posture were relaxed. The medicine was obviously relieving her pain, but it was worrying that she now took additional doses during the day.

"Join us," Juliana invited. "I need your ideas for my garden. I want a womanly retreat from all the male influence on this ranch."

Don León chuckled. "The male influence is what will pay for your womanly garden."

Anna studied the sketch with them for several minutes and asked questions about the plantings. "Perhaps a small reflecting pool?" she asked.

"Oh, yes," said Juliana. "Put it in the center, León, and draw paths radiating out at angles. I want the garden to contain twists and turns and surprises."

"Where one could get lost in the dark," Anna added. The women laughed together.

Don León nodded and said, "We'll dig the pool and line it with dark clay. A buried water line and some stonework can make it look like a natural spring."

A few deft lines and the pool and winding pathways were in place. He laid down his pen and took Juliana's hand. Her expression became wary.

Looking into her eyes, he said, "At last, I can offer a dwelling fit for my beautiful wife. A house to furnish inspiration and magic for her soul."

Such tender words, but Juliana's face turned to stone. Anna quickly found an excuse to withdraw. She paced about her room. How would it feel to be loved by such a sensitive man? He offered Juliana everything except the one thing that could make her happy.

She stood by the window, fingering her crucifix. Don León was an intelligent man. Why could he not see that his words of devotion held no meaning for Juliana as long as he refused to consider adoption?

I must be missing something vital. She wasn't privy to their private exchanges.

The next morning Juliana shared deeper bitterness. "I don't believe him, Anna, when he says he doesn't want to adopt a child because it might be too much for my fragile health. I think if he cannot have a child of his own he doesn't want any at all."

Not that again. "You say that, but his expression and his words tell a different story. I believe he loves you too much to risk losing you. He seems unaware of class lines. He is unfailingly kind to me and I have no status at all."

Juliana's lips tightened. "Don't argue when you

have no understanding. I am tired of you defending him. You're different. With your background it's easy to accept you as one of the family. You don't know him as I do."

"I'll say no more, Juliana. I merely hoped to reassure you."

If only she really were part of the family. The role of servant, for the first time, felt overly burdensome. Forever at the beck and call of Juliana, a woman who was one minute smiling and the next in a huff. Did she really want to spend the rest of her life as a companion to this woman?

She couldn't see a better alternative. And the thought of leaving was not appealing. Had she locked herself in a golden cage?

Anna rejoiced in watching springtime lay a mantle of green over the countryside. The work on the house was progressing well. March melted into April's song, but Anna's heart grew heavier for her employers. A worrisome change had occurred in the conflict between Juliana and her long-suffering husband.

Don León spent less and less time with Juliana. He left soon after breakfast on most days and did not return until just before dinner, pleading that he had been with workmen gathering materials and staking out changes.

If he ate with the women, he remained preoccupied and silent. Gone were the interesting stories of a day's happenings. Many evenings he took his dinner alone in the library. Juliana didn't speak of his absence, but the angry lines etched on her face revealed her feelings.

Their salvation was the garden. Juliana and Anna collaborated on fine weather days, laying out beds and sketching pathways in the soil. One morning Don León joined them. They stood watching him supervise workmen placing adobe bricks on a lengthening wall.

"The footprint of the house is nearly three times that of the original, so the outer garden walls must grow accordingly," he said.

"No doubt it will be grand." Juliana's voice held a dangerous note. "I've never understood why you insist on such a big house for only the two of us."

Don León stared at her for a moment, shook his head, and continued as if she hadn't spoken. "The garden will feature both native plants and some from our Spanish homeland: olive, palm, and citrus trees. They'll provide shade and variety, but be positioned to leave open vistas of the house."

He smiled down at Anna. "I intend to bring those three large century plants we saw growing on the hillside near the orchard. Put them in the back corner. They're giants, Juliana. You'll enjoy the contrast to your smaller plantings."

"In my garden? You said I could use my own ideas." Juliana plopped down on a garden bench and drew off her gloves.

Anna swallowed hard. What could she say?

Don León flexed his gloved fingers and droned on. "Creating a garden is about creating joy. A garden of flowers and foliage should also be a garden of thoughts and dreams."

Anna tried to cover Juliana's silence. "My mother said, 'Plant a garden for one's nose and the eyes are satisfied.' As a child I enjoyed working in the garden because I could get dirty without a scolding."

Don León and Juliana both managed smiles. "I find I can bury a lot of troubles digging in the dirt," he said, watching Juliana.

She glared up at him. "That does not work for me." Her mouth tightened and she rose and stalked away.

Don León kicked at a clod of dirt, his brows drawn down. Anna sent him an apologetic glance and followed Juliana to the library.

"His books should be good for something. Help me find a vine to plant along the new wall. I want it to cover the arched gateway into my garden and add color."

Anna's research revealed the beauty and medicinal uses of blue-flowered *passiflora,* or passion flowers.

"Perfect," Juliana said. "León said I could choose whatever I want for my garden. It's his job to find them."

She returned to the garden and issued her orders. "And, León, I want that big cypress near the front gate moved into my garden."

"It will be difficult to move such a large tree, but I'll see to it—and locate your passion flowers."

Juliana's face transformed with her beautiful smile, and Don León planted a kiss on her forehead.

But two days later, only Don León and Anna supervised the work on Juliana's garden. Despite Anna's pleading, she refused to come outdoors.

"You two don't need me. Your ideas flow along the same lines. I want a nap. Give me another dose of my medicine before you go, and send María to massage my neck."

Anna trudged out to join Don León as he supervised the transplanting of the large cypress from its spot near the front gate to a location near the pool. He stood, hands on his hips, watching several workmen lower the great tree into place.

"She should be here. It's her garden." His voice was hard.

"It's a good spot for the cypress, Don León. The pond will mirror the tree's graceful lines but its debris won't fall into the water."

The informal Spanish he insisted she use still felt awkward on Anna's tongue. With Juliana it had been easier. But he was the master of the house. It wasn't polite to speak to him so casually. She wasn't family and he was years older. Mamá would not have approved.

"You planned the site, Anna. I believe the garden is more important to you than to Juliana. I'm going to get her."

Anna watched him stride away. The garden had become important to her. Too important? The work kept her from worrying, but Juliana's attitude was wearing thin. Why couldn't she appreciate the amazing man who was her husband?

The women dined alone again that night. After dinner, Anna read from the scriptures while Juliana picked at her needlework. Perhaps the truths from God's word would sink into her troubled soul. She had so much to live for: a man who gave in to her on every issue but one. But oh, that one! She was obsessed.

Juliana set aside her needlework and began to pace the room. "You don't understand him as I do, Anna. He bears a deep pride of his aristocratic name, and I believe he's unwilling to share it with anyone from a lesser background. I've come to believe my status attracted him more than my soul."

Anna dropped her head and closed her eyes. Words were useless. "Will you pray with me?"

Juliana shook her head. "Futile. God won't hear me since I'm unable or unwilling to confess my sins."

What would happen? Juliana's precarious health couldn't hold up against such stress.

"I may as well be single. León sits in his *oficina*, night after night, drinking brandy and poring over house plans, while you and I sit alone. You heard the footman admit the plate on Leó's desk was untouched."

It was best not to answer. She'd read it as defense of Don León. The lump in Anna's throat made it difficult to swallow.

Juliana sighed. "I almost forgot to tell you. María will need your help tomorrow packing for the move. León says the new guest house is almost complete. You'll stay there with us until the renovations are finished, but María will remain in her same quarters. She can help in the kitchens."

Anna pressed her lips together. Would she have any time to herself in the small house? She'd become accustomed to slipping away to the kitchen for coffee and common-sense discussions with Ramona.

"Antonio will supervise the move," Juliana continued, "since he's the only one León trusts." She drained her wine glass. "If only he treasured his wife as much as his possessions."

Anna fingered her crucifix. At least she would have Antonio's welcome company for several days. Don León had kept him too busy for rides with her in the past two weeks.

"Call María. Watch as she massages my neck, Anna. That will be your job now. And bring me another dose of the medicine."

"Juliana, the doctor said—"

"I know what the doctor said, but the pain in my head and neck are intense. I'll never be able to sleep."

After María left, Anna sat in the chair beside Juliana's bed until she slept. Two doses of medicine during the daytime and now a doubled dose at night. Too much. She must tell Don León. But when would she see him?

Eleven

Juliana's indecision made the packing much more difficult than Anna had envisioned. When Antonio and another *vaquero* arrived to carry the trunks Anna and María had just packed, Anna pasted on a smile.

"I'm sorry, Antonio. You'll need to bring back the first two you moved. Juliana says they must be emptied and repacked because she can't remember what was in them." Anna shook her head, but Antonio only winked at her and smiled.

By the third day Juliana had reduced María to tears, saying she dawdled.

"Juliana, she's moving as fast as you allow. She packs a dress and you have her unpack it." Anna stopped—too late. The words had been spoken.

Juliana's eyebrows rose and she stared at Anna, her eyes cold. After a long pause she laughed. "I'm not good at decisions."

Anna managed a smile. What was she thinking? A servant did not criticize her employer. Juliana's temper was unpredictable. She might dismiss Anna on the spot. The choice to leave, if and when she was ready, should be Anna's.

The next afternoon the packing outpaced workmen putting finishing touches on the guesthouse. No room for more trunks. Anna rode with Antonio while Juliana napped with María by her side.

Antonio lifted Anna from the saddle at the top of a foothill overlooking the hacienda a couple of miles away. He swept his hand out to call attention to what lay below.

"One of my favorite views."

"It's lovely, Antonio: the sparkle of the river below, the intense green of the orchards beyond, and the house in the distance. Almost as beautiful to me as the coastline. The ocean seems to be in my blood. When swells break into crowns of white spray, my spirit soars."

His eyes sparkled. "The daughter of a sea-faring man should have salt water in her veins. For me, it's this." He motioned again. "I'm as much a part of this land as the soil. I feed on its ruggedness and the challenge of pitting myself against wild cattle. They can be subdued, but never really tamed."

He looked the part—strong and fit. He pushed his hat back on its string and wiped his brow with the kerchief at his neck. His dark, wavy hair, reaching almost to his shoulders, ruffled in the breeze. He'd never looked more appealing.

"I sense it, Antonio—the powerful hold these ranges have on you."

His stallion stamped, ready to move on. Antonio patted the animal's flank. "The ranch is my home. I was born here. My father trained me on these ranges. I know no other life. I expect to die here."

"I, too, have come to love this ranch. I'm surrounded by horses and cattle, the men who care for them, and the women who care for the men. A familiar life. I want to stay forever."

Antonio's gaze became intense. "Do you ever think of marriage? You're a very beautiful woman. A woman to bring out the best in a man."

Her eyes widened. Color rose in his face before he looked away. His remark opened a whole new vein of thought. Was Antonio interested in her as a woman?

She offered, "Juliana told me about the death of your family. I know how loss feels." Was he ready to think of another union?

His discomfiture disappeared, and with it, his hint at marriage. He took her hand for a moment. "Your grief is more recent than mine. Yet you've moved on, ready to take the next step God reveals. It took me longer. I did not expect ever to be happy again after Elena and the children died. In truth, not even to find a reason to live; but Don León challenged my grief."

"What did he do?"

"After watching me grieve for the better part of a year, León came to me. Instead of sympathy he offered me the opportunity to work alongside him as his second-in-command."

"A perfect choice, Antonio. Your skills are unsurpassed."

He smiled. "I'm not sure of that, but Don León shared his heart with me for the first time. 'Together,' he said, 'we'll give legs to my vision. My father's plan for the hacienda was too small. He's gone now. You and I can create an empire. You're the man I trust to manage the cattle and leave me free to oversee new hemp plantations and a fiber factory. Then, who knows? Together we'll build an enterprise beyond my father's wildest expectations.'"

"And you did, Antonio. You helped him create the largest hacienda in Monterey, with its working ranch and extensive hemp plantations. De Montaraz products are shipped to Mexico City and even to ports in Europe. Don León's trust was well placed. You are quite a man, Antonio Rivera." She smiled up at him. "Do you think he will ever stop expanding his empire?"

"Not until his last breath. Grasping at the biggest prize has never been important to me, but loyalty is. Don León has always been more than fair with me. I accepted the position of *caporal* and have given him my best efforts since that day. I caught a whiff of the fever that drove him and worked tirelessly beside him. I empathized with his obsession for an heir, and grieved with him through the deaths of two still-born sons. It's what a friend does."

"Sad there will be no de Montaraz heir." Anna looked deep into Antonio's eyes. Something stirred inside her. She hoped to feel the gentle touch of his hand again. Antonio was strong and dependable. A man of faith, well able to weather adversity. Would he ever love again?

He said, "Perhaps we should return."

Anna wanted to hold him back. To learn more about the man who stood before her: what he expected in a woman, and whether he was interested in her. But the moment had been lost.

On the return ride Anna replayed Antonio's words. "A woman to bring out the best in a man."

Am I really such a woman? Her thinking had changed. She was no longer ready to settle for a marriage of convenience and wait for a love that might or might not develop. She wanted to be in love with her man before she married him—to be eagerly awaiting the union. *Is that man Antonio?*

When they reached the house, he smiled up at her and held out his arms, ready to help her dismount. "I promised Ramona to bring you for a visit and a cup of coffee."

On the kitchen terrace, Ramona joined Anna and Antonio. He soon had the women laughing with the story of his one try at bread-making in Ramona's kitchen.

A gentle man, unafraid to laugh at himself. One to consider if he pursues me.

Anna's gaze followed him as he went for the coffee pot. As he disappeared, Don León's unhappy face intruded into her thoughts. Antonio was as wise as Ramona. Perhaps he could offer advice about the stressful situation between her employers.

Anna caught Ramona staring at her. The cook ducked her head and said, "May I speak frankly, Anna?"

At her nod, Ramona continued, "I think of you as the daughter I never had, although we come from very different backgrounds. Do you trust me?"

"Oh, I trust your wisdom as I do few people. I treasure our friendship."

Ramona reached for Anna's hand. "I see Juliana's untouched plates and Don León's. I see the worry on your face, but Antonio cannot advise you, if that is your hope. Don León is a proud man, accustomed to giving orders, not asking for advice."

Anna's cheeks heated. Was she so transparent, worried as she was? Her caring for both of her employers drove her to new boldness.

"I'm astounded, Ramona. You're not only wise, you must be a mind-reader."

Ramona chuckled. "You aren't hard to read. Your face gives away your thoughts."

"I'm glad you understand the problem, Ramona. I wanted to tell you before now." She chewed at her lip. "I've never seen two more unhappy people. Don León is, perhaps, the more miserable. He drinks too much and has withdrawn from her. Juliana doesn't seem to care."

"I'm sorry Doña Juliana dragged you into their conflict. It surfaces now and again. Then they rub along in peace for a while. Don't take sides, Anna. Try to persuade her to speak to Fray Serra. It's a spiritual problem those two share. Each has too much pride to compromise."

Something else showed in Ramona's expression. "What are you holding back, Ramona?"

"You're concerned about the wrong man. Instead of worrying about Don León, think about this man who has become your friend. A man who—"

Antonio appeared in the doorway, coffee pot in hand. What would Ramona have added? Anna held out her cup but didn't look up at Antonio, flustered that he may have heard Ramona's words. He would think she'd been pressing for information about him.

He began talking about Don León's plans to buy still more rangeland in the Carmel Valley. "He says one day, as more people come to California, land

100

will be worth far more than even he can imagine. The countryside is filled with riches. Even now France and England are trying to encroach with their fur hunters and explorers."

"I feed them more often now. Rough men—always hungry," Ramona said. "And a few adventurers from the colonies that threw off the control of England and formed their own nation."

"The *Americanos*—they're the biggest threat. The Spanish Empire is weakening. Don León predicts it will be every man for himself in a few years. Only the strongest will survive."

"Frightening," Anna said. "Although I can understand why people will want to come to this beautiful land."

"And we can't expect them to get along. Greed is not pretty."

She studied Antonio, focusing on his strong features and gentle voice. But, as happened so often now, her thoughts slid to Don León. He may not want it, but he needed Antonio's wise counsel. Did the two ever speak of spiritual matters? Even Fray Serra seemed uncertain of Don León's faith.

His stress over the missing heir must be greater than Juliana's. He not only worried about his wife's health, but faced an uncertain future for the Spanish heritage so dear to him. All he had worked for could be stripped away without a strong heir to manage the hacienda when he was gone.

That evening Juliana picked at the slice of succulent roast beef on her tray and scowled. She'd refused to get out of bed to dine. Anna narrowed her eyes as Juliana pushed the plate aside. "Tasteless. Read to me from the scriptures."

Psalms usually lifted Anna's spirit. She chose one from an old Bible Don León had loaned her. After a few verses Juliana held up a trembling hand.

"I feel even worse. God is angry with me. Punishing my weak faith by denying me children."

Anna closed her eyes. She was at wit's end.

Juliana balled up the linen napkin and threw it to the floor. "I'm useless to León if I cannot have children. He wants a son more than I do. His empire has no heir."

Exactly. But he treasures you even above his desire for an heir.

"Can't you take a few more bites? You're losing weight you can't spare."

"Nonsense, Anna." Juliana tossed her head. "I've threatened to live apart from him and still he refuses to adopt. I'll do whatever it takes. I *will* have a child." Juliana's scowl deepened. "Why will he not let me try again or find me one?"

Anna's eyes glazed. *Back on that vein.* "You seem to forget I'm an unlikely confidante to the master of the house."

"He respects you. Enjoys your company." Her voice sharpened. "I sometimes think you favor him over me."

Anna put her hand on Juliana's arm. "I love you both as my family." It was true, but Juliana could be so unreasonable. Don León, on the other hand...

Juliana blinked and her voice softened. "Pay no attention to me. I appreciate your loyalty and friendship. I'm wrong to burden you with our problems. León would be furious if he knew, but I have nowhere else to turn."

If only Juliana would confer with someone of real wisdom. "Won't you consult Fray Serra?"

"Never. He would be shocked to learn our marriage has deteriorated into a struggle over a child. And don't speak to him yourself. The problem is mine."

Fray Serra's reaction to a confession from her would not be shock. He would have heard worse.

"Ramona made your favorites. Please eat something. You'll sleep better."

Juliana clenched her fork and took a few desultory bites before she asked Anna to refill her wine glass. "He drinks brandy for hours, closed away from me in his office. When he finally comes to our quarters he carries another glass out to the terrace until he's certain I'm asleep. León wishes I would die."

"No, Juliana. Don León is obviously out of his mind with worry."

"Good. Perhaps he'll give me my way." She yawned. "I'm ready for bed. Brush my hair for me and massage my neck. No need for María. You do it better. And bring fresh pillows. I've wallowed in these all day."

Anna lay awake for hours. Juliana was becoming intolerable with her tantrums and her physical expectations. The tension was sure to escalate in the tiny guest house with Anna glued to Juliana's bedside.

Is my safe harbor worth the loss of my self-respect?

Twelve

The guest house had only a tiny kitchen and a sunny breakfast room. María brought meals from the *casa principal*, where the large kitchens and servant quarters would remain unchanged. After three days, Anna found herself preparing a simple breakfast for the couple when María failed to bring food.

What could have happened to Ramona's usual efficiency? Anna rolled up her sleeves. She could manage alone. She'd been in the kitchen often enough as a child, wheedling treats and admiring the cooks' deft preparations.

The last sprinkles of an early-morning April shower dampened Anna's hair as she dashed toward the cool-storage hut. Inside, beside its cool, bubbling spring, she selected the remnants of a ham, a few eggs, and a slab of butter.

Back in the kitchen, she busied herself boiling water for eggs, and calculating how much coffee to use. What would Porfirio think of the sister he had dismissed as useless?

Don León had not yet appeared when Anna carried a tray to Juliana. She'd refused to get out of bed to eat with her husband.

"Juice and toast, Juliana, and a slice of ham." Anna propped pillows behind her back and at her sides to support the wooden tray. "Please eat and then you can have a nap. I know you didn't sleep well."

Juliana had begun coughing in the night and complained of difficulty in breathing. She called for Anna, saying her chest hurt and she wanted an extra dose of medication. Anna had noted Don León's absence at the time, but supposed him still in his office.

This morning Juliana's face was clear. She leaned back with a surprising smile and a show of strength. Underneath Anna sensed frailty, ready to drag her down again.

"Don't fuss so, Anna. I'm all right. I just need rest. Go and have your breakfast."

"Will you walk in the garden with me if you nap for an hour?"

"We'll see. The night was a torment. The medication stopped my cough, but I didn't sleep and neither did León. I told him I'd be better in here alone. He only shrugged and said he'd sleep on the cot in the pantry. He doesn't care, Anna."

But what fresh pain did you bring to him? A man wants his wife beside him. Anna bit back words she longed to say: "Tell your husband his love is important to you. More important even than having a child." If only Juliana would give a little. Don León was a strong and prideful man.

Juliana finished half a piece of toast and a few swallows of juice. "Bring me another dose. I'll have a nap and then, perhaps, a walk with you."

Another idle promise. There would be no walk. Anna carried the tray back to the kitchen and hacked at the cold ham with trembling hands. She nicked her finger and the knife slipped from her hand and fell to the floor. She poured water over her bleeding finger. She *must* speak to Don León. Juliana needed food and fresh air, not medication.

Before now it had felt kinder to talk about the garden and keep his mind away from the problems of his wife, but Anna was frightened. Juliana might die. And the medication was only making things worse.

While she struggled to tie a clean rag strip around her finger, Don León entered the kitchen. He helped her with the bandage. "Is it a bad cut?"

"No, only a nick."

He looked as immaculate as ever, but his hand shook as he lifted the cup she offered. Too much brandy last night? He didn't ask about Juliana.

He picked up the fallen knife. "Here, let me help," he said. "I've cooked over campfires, so we can manage." He found another knife and sliced the ham and a few pieces of bread. "You might set the table, Anna, and drop the eggs to boil."

The two bumped into each other in the tiny space, but they soon had a meal ready. As she set the table, Anna offered a desperate prayer for wisdom.

When they were seated, she forced herself to look at Don León. It was difficult to ignore his tender smile. "I must tell you how concerned I am—" Her voice wavered and she cleared her throat. "I'm concerned for Doña Juliana. She sleeps much more often now, and her appetite is non-existent. She uses too much medication, and she will not listen to reason."

Don León's shoulders slumped. He took a sip of coffee. "I know, Anna. She refuses my advice—even my company. But the doctor assures me her despair will pass. Once the house is complete, I believe she'll recover in the new surroundings."

When Anna didn't reply, he pointed to her plate. "Please eat. I'm as concerned for you as for my wife. I regret the difficulties she causes you. Juliana is capable of selfishness."

Anna picked at her food. "She ate only a few bites of her dinner last night, and this morning even less. Then she demanded more medication. I feel helpless, Don León." Her voice shook, but she had to make him see. "Juliana has no interest in going out of doors, even in this fine weather. I don't know what her cough means. She may be truly ill. I don't have the experience to care for her. She needs a real nurse. Perhaps I should leave."

Tears flooded her eyes. She excused herself and fled to the kitchen. She startled as Don León's strong arms enwrapped her.

"Don't cry, Anna. You do everything you can— certainly more than I do. I've given up trying to make her happy. Her words to me are bitter, and she won't allow me to touch her. You are my only hope. Please don't leave." A soft sob escaped his lips. Don León pulled her head onto his shoulder.

Anna pushed away from him to wipe her cheeks. Their eyes met. The moment lengthened. He cupped her chin and lifted her mouth to his into a tender kiss. Her arms were about his neck before she could stop them.

Anna tore herself away. "Don León..." She tried to catch her breath "I apologize. Please sit down and I will reheat your food." She returned the coffee pot to the brazier.

He laid his hand on her shoulder. "Look at me, Anna. I'm the one who should beg forgiveness. You did nothing wrong." His gaze seemed to reach down into her heart, holding a sadness that aged him. "But I cannot find it in me to regret the only comfort I've had in many months. I won't require any breakfast this morning. Just see to Juliana, please." He strode from the kitchen.

The next day, relief rolled over Anna like fog gently drifting off the ocean. Ramona had sent word that Don León would stay in the big house and take his meals there. She wouldn't have to face him. It was hard enough with Juliana.

Guilt churned each time she replayed the feel of his strong arms around her and the taste of his lips. She should have refused to let him hold her, let alone answered his kiss. The blame was hers alone.

What if Juliana saw them? Improbable, but the kiss was wrong—so very wrong. If only she could seek Fray Serra's wisdom and cleanse her conscience. Even if she could, would it be right to betray Don León's one weak moment? He had been caught up in her emotional storm. She must find the right solution to this precarious development on her own. Anna whispered another prayer.

Juliana's demands became a welcome distraction, although it meant being confined in the guest house. She'd decided she wanted Anna to stay by her bedside even when she slept.

"The medication makes me dizzy but it relieves the pain and helps me nap. I need you beside me, just in case."

Looking into Anna's disapproving expression, Juliana added, "I know I'm taking more than the doctor prescribed, but I'm the judge of how I feel, so say no more about doctor's orders."

It wasn't until the end of the week that Anna could slip away to the kitchen. She found Ramona up to her dimpled elbows in floury dough.

"Sorry about the morning your food wasn't delivered," Ramona huffed. "María was ill and a new footman—" She shrugged.

The usual knot formed in Anna's chest as she remembered that morning. "Of no consequence, Ramona. I managed." She accepted a mug of chocolate and pulled up a stool.

"Juliana sleeps most of the day now. Don León is as bewildered as I am. The doctor has come twice in the past three days. He brought a milder sleeping medication but she takes it even more often."

Ramona shook her head. "For years Doña Juliana has had problems sleeping. She isn't active enough. I thank God for the work that keeps me strong and ready to appreciate rest." As if to demonstrate her words, Ramona hefted a tall can of milk from the floor to the counter.

"It's out of my hands. Juliana sent for María this morning when I refused to give more medication than the doctor prescribed. María will do Juliana's bidding. I've failed in my duties."

Ramona patted her hand. "Don't worry. She went into a similar decline two years ago, and recovered, stronger than before. We'll ask God to take this."

If only she could tell Ramona everything. Don León's anguish had driven him into Anna's arms and she'd kissed another woman's husband. Sin had multiplied in the small house, but she couldn't seek relief. She must keep her employers' secrets.

Juliana had what every woman desired. She was beautiful. Security, significance, and intimacy, if she chose, were wrapped in the handsome package of her husband. Anna decided Juliana needed no one — only a willing provider for whatever she desired at the moment.

The following day seemed to prove her right. Juliana moved María into the cottage and dismissed Anna, saying she could sleep in the *casa principal*. "I need María with me at night. You can take over her duties in the kitchens until I'm well. Ramona can use the help."

"Whatever you say, Juliana. I'll be near if you decide you need me."

Should she leave? Pride over practicality? Leaving meant leaving the hacienda and Ramona and Antonio. They had become very dear. She shouldn't have to give them up for the whim of a capricious woman. Don León had employed her. He should make the final decision.

She still cared for Juliana. They'd shared many fine hours. Perhaps, as Juliana said, the parting would be brief. Or perhaps she would demand a permanent dismissal.

A week passed. Anna welcomed the exhausting kitchen tasks. The work kept her from worrying, and Ramona's cheerful outlook lifted her spirits. They shared Ramona's cottage. Anna had a small bed there.

They spent time outdoors, and on three evenings, Antonio joined them. Anna could feel herself mending.

Another week slid by before Don León's serious face appeared at the window in late afternoon. "We must talk, Señorita. Come ride with me."

"Please give me a few minutes before I join you at the *corrales*."

Don León nodded and strode away. With a heavy sensation in her chest, Anna finished her task and pulled Ramona aside.

"Juliana sent him to do a job she dreaded. She has had time to reflect and has come to resent me. María won't argue with her about the medication. He means to dismiss me."

Had Porfirio been right all along? Perhaps she was a useless ornament, unfit to succeed on her own.

No. I will not fall into that trap. I will find a way to succeed. I must.

"Fray Serra told me I could help in the mission school, but I know nothing of children. I wonder if I'll be any more successful there."

"Don't try to do God's job, Anna. Only He can see the future. I've known Don León all his life. He's a fair and honest man. Ride with him and see what he has to say."

They rode to a spot overlooking the Carmel River. Don León helped her dismount, then removed the *serape* he kept rolled behind his saddle. It became a warm poncho when needed, but today he spread it over a flat rock near the river's edge and bid her sit before he returned to his saddle bag.

"I brought a flask of wine." He filled small silver cups and offered one. "To relax us." His face was inscrutable, but his voice was warm.

Anna held the cup, fingers trembling, and sipped. Don León had shown only kindness in all the time she'd known him. Powerful man that he was, he was concerned for her, a servant in his household.

Her cheeks warmed under his steady gaze. In the tawny light his eyes were the color of the river. She looked away and pointed to a heron near the far bank, waiting to spear his dinner. Don León grinned and tossed a pebble. The bird lifted with the splash and Anna smiled.

"I'm always fascinated with the elegant motions that mark a heron's flight," he said.

They were silent for a while. Finally he spoke. "My office is complete. The stained glass window you and Juliana designed adds a perfect touch. I think the work on the *casa principal* will be finished before Christmas."

He was skirting the issue, dreading the task before him. An evening breeze ruffled Anna's hair, carrying with it the smells of the river. She still couldn't look at Don León. She focused on the green of corn stalks in a field beyond the rushing water, and swallows hawking for insects above it.

A gentle ending to my life at the hacienda. I'll be forever grateful to him.

Don León leaned toward her. "I miss seeing you, Anna. You didn't deserve what Juliana did."

"There's no need to pretend, Don León. I know you came to dismiss me. I was unequal to the task. I've failed you and Juliana."

He shook his head. "You failed at nothing. Juliana is in one of her pouts, but it will pass and she'll want you with her again."

Anna swallowed around the lump in her throat and pretended to study the dying sun's scarlet dance on the water. Did she wish to return to her duties with Juliana? Fray Serra believed God had purpose for her at the hacienda, but he'd accept her decision to leave if she chose.

Don León's voice, warm and soft, interrupted her thoughts. "There's no need for you to toil in the kitchens while you await reinstatement. The work is too heavy."

"I'm not certain I want reinstatement. Fray Serra said he can use me in the mission school. I need to consult him."

His eyes widened and he drew an audible breath. "You mustn't leave us! We need you. Please say you won't leave. Besides, I believe the good friar is away at another mission for a few weeks."

"I must do what is right." She took another sip of wine, grateful for the soothing warmth it spread. She let the silence lengthen.

"I've recently finished building a cottage a short distance upriver, Anna. You can live there and plant a garden of your own. Let me take care of you for a while. Rest while you decide how to shape your life. I feel responsible. You would not be in this predicament if I'd not brought you here."

"I welcomed your offer of employment, Don León. It was a godsend."

Time to rest and reflect. No conflict.

There was latent risk to the new offer. Still, Fray Serra believed in the honor of Don León, as did as Ramona and Antonio. Perhaps he truly thought of her as family. It should be safe enough. The kiss had not been his fault.

"I try to follow God's precepts, Don León. Juliana might misunderstand."

He watched her for a moment and took her hand. "I care about you as a friend. Juliana has been deliberately cruel to both of us. I'm a lonely man, Anna. We can help each other heal. I promise I'll ask you for nothing more than you think it right to give. Trust me."

Thirteen

Anna had been living in the cozy little cottage for almost a month. About a mile from the *casa principal*, it was tucked away among some large sycamore trees just inside the mouth of a canyon. A small stream trickled its way behind the property and several large oaks shaded the creek. A small barn was filled with hay, and Consuelo occupied its stable yard, ready to carry Anna to her work in the kitchens. Anna's garden thrived in the May sun.

A curious peace pervaded, a sense of things working in their proper courses. None of the upsets and turmoil of service to Juliana.

Today, as all others, Anna did light chores in the kitchen and returned to her house after lunch. His orders. Ramona's sweet face had invited confidences. She must wonder at the change in circumstances, but Anna couldn't share what she didn't understand.

When she reached the cottage, she rested on her luxurious bed and read in one of the books León had brought. He was León now. Friends did not use titles.

She was waiting on the garden bench when he arrived at sunset for his daily visit, carrying a parcel. Anna greeted him and asked, as she did each day, "Has Juliana spoken about my return?"

"The day will come. Let's not speak of my wife. Juliana sleeps too much of the time, but it's pointless to worry. She talks only to the doctor. It seems she still has no use for either of us."

Anna shook her head. "And what of Antonio? I haven't seen him in the kitchen in weeks. Of course he wouldn't think it proper to visit me here alone."

León rubbed at an ear. "My fault, I suppose. I'm keeping him busier than usual, sending him to take care of affairs I usually supervise. I've been staying near the house in case you or Juliana need me."

He held out the parcel. "I brought you something for your kitchen table. This little house must be dark at night."

Anna unwrapped two silver candlesticks. "They're lovely, León, but I cannot accept them. You've already given me a mirror for my dresser."

"Because a hand mirror will not suffice for anyone so lovely." He smiled that smile that made her heart bounce.

"And a garden bench."

"A place for us to sit and discuss the books you're reading."

"From your library, León. You're far too generous." She felt her cheeks color. "I seem to be unable to say no to you when you come suggesting a ride, or when you kneel beside me in the garden, weeding my flowers and vegetables. Is it really proper for the two of us to spend so much time alone?"

"We're friends, Anna. I receive pleasure from your company and from bringing you simple things. I'll never ask anything in return." He held out his hand. "What about a ride to see the new calves? This year's crop is a good one."

He was so convincing. And she looked forward to his visits and the long rides they shared. They could speak so freely. She enjoyed his company—perhaps too much.

He's a friend like no other. Something niggled inside her at the thought, and the sense of rightness diminished. She needed to reexamine their relationship.

As Anna watered her flowers the next afternoon, she thought about León—again. A gentle man, he was careful of her position as a single woman. No inappropriate words or touches, but an undercurrent had developed between them. Something inside her had unfurled to bask in his appreciation.

She needed to admit the truth. He was forever on her mind. How had she allowed it to happen? León de Montaraz had become the man of her long-ago dreams. But he must remain a dream out of reach.

I love him.

Her shoulders stiffened and she raised her head to listen. Had she spoken aloud? Only the sounds of a lazy spring afternoon met her ears: the hum of a bee working near her, the trill of a lark, the bark of one of the shepherds' dogs in the distance. In the deep blue dome of the sky above her, clouds piled heavenward in the late afternoon heat.

She took off her hat and wiped her brow. An honesty born of the moment compelled her to say again what she had not dared admit to herself before.

"I am in love with León." Anna said the words aloud, hoping the exposure would shock her into sanity, but they sounded reasonable.

Reasonable? He was Juliana's husband.

"I can't help myself. What woman would not love him?" León de Montaraz—supportive, charming, and so willing to meet her needs. She sat back and clasped her knees. Her hands trembled.

No! But her mind echoed, "It's true. You're in love with León."

In following days when wisdom prevailed in her inner arguments, Anna resolved to leave. The next day, at the end of the week—always in the near future. But how could she tell him? What reason could she give? It was easier to stay. She felt protected here. Life could be good if she was careful. And she could see León. The proverbial forbidden fruit.

He would never learn from her that she loved him. She would not betray her faith or Juliana. She and León didn't speak of personal feelings. They discussed lofty ideas from his books and talked of the ranch. Things important to both of them. She could remain his special friend. He had become her anchor. Her link to security and a life she wanted. And he said he needed her.

Anna pushed away a darkening suspicion that León had developed an attachment for her. She could see the signs, but they were both honorable people. They could steer around any pitfalls. As he said, they completed each other and they harmed no one.

One night in early June, Anna and León enjoyed

an evening ride through the countryside and a picnic beside the river. It was later than usual when they returned to the cottage. León entered the cottage ahead of her. He bent to light the silver candlesticks in a place of pride atop her small kitchen table.

"You were right," she said. "The cottage was dark before you brought them." Her eyes readjusted to the glow and she smiled up at him. "Thank you, León. A wonderful evening."

He didn't reply. He held a candlestick at chest level and his chiseled jaw cast a shadow on his upper face. He stood, still and silent. She could feel his intent gaze. He raised the candlestick and she looked at him for an instant, then shrank from what she saw in his eyes. Her body shook. She could not, would not, go against God's will. Another nervous peek. He still watched her.

"León?" Embarrassed by the quaver in her voice, she tried for nonchalance. "I'll see you tomorrow. Ramona is teaching me to make *tortillas de harina*. I'll save my best effort for you."

He set the candlestick on the table and pulled her to him, caressing her shoulders and arms. He kissed the top of her head. His voice, muffled in her hair, pleaded, "Juliana has cast us both out. I'm lonely, Anna. Make me the happiest man in the world, and be with me." His voice was strained, taut.

She raised her face. "León, this is not—"

His lips found hers and she melted against him, even as her mind clamored a warning. She managed a half-hearted push against his chest and he raised his lips.

"*Querida*, it's meant to be. Why else would you come to this ranch of all places on the earth? I'll make it right. I promise to find a way. We need each other. Let me stay."

He kissed along her neck, then raised his head. She felt his fingers at the clasp of her crucifix. "In my way," he muttered. "This sweet spot belongs to me."

She heard the clink of the necklace against the tiled tabletop. "No. I never take it off—"

He lifted her from the floor, murmuring as he carried her toward the bed. Anna lay back in his arms for a moment, then tried to sit again. His smile was gentle. "Don't be afraid, my love."

Blood rushed to her brain and she knew. This was surrender. Fear of the forbidden gave way to the thrill of his need. His tender words and touches silenced the voice inside her. When his breathing slowed and she judged him asleep, she shed tears. She turned her back and inched away, trying to control them, but a sob shook her.

León snuggled against her. "Anna?" he whispered.

She couldn't answer. He turned her toward him and she covered her face. He pulled her hands down, kissed them, and wiped a tear. He pulled her close. "I hurt you. I meant to be gentle and patient, dearest one, but you're so exciting and I was lost in my need."

Moonlight poured through the window. She could see his troubled face. "No, León. You don't understand—"

He put his finger to her lips. "Don't spare me, *querida*. It will never happen again. Please forgive me."

"You didn't hurt me, León. That's not why I cry."

His face relaxed. "Ah. I understand, *amada*. An emotional moment in a woman's life. It comes but once.

I'll treasure the gift you gave me as I treasure you. I find you exhilarating, yet I'm at peace in your presence." He shifted her head to his shoulder and stroked her hair.

He didn't understand at all, but what could she say? Later, he lay tousled and spent on the pillow beside her, his dark-fringed eyelids closed; but sleep eluded her. She touched the curve of his beautiful mouth and straightened the sheet dragged sideways across his muscular chest. A flush of heat coursed through her when he stirred.

She'd never forget what followed. The emptiness and chill when León slipped from bed and his gentle parting kiss as she pretended to sleep. He moved about, fumbling in the darkened room for his clothing, and she watched him tiptoe away.

As soon as it was light, Anna stripped the soiled sheets from the bed and tore them into ribbons. She kindled a blaze and stuffed them into the fireplace. The laundresses must not see them.

Something gleamed on the table in a single ray of the sun. Her crucifix—the one Father gave her to remind her that God is always near. She picked it up and hid it in the box that held Father's ring. She closed the drawer and looked up to see a pale face in the mirror.

The daughter of righteous parents. A child of God. León is Juliana's husband. Something withered inside and she broke. She flung herself onto the unmade bed and cried until she had no more tears. When she rose she knew what she must do.

He came that evening, his face alight at the sight of her, and Anna delivered the words.

León aged before her eyes. "I'll stay away if that's what you want. I cannot imagine how, but I will. I never meant to cause you pain, *preciosa*. It was the only way I knew to show how much I love you."

She couldn't watch him leave. The door closed and she stood rooted to the spot, praying that her feet would not run after him. She cried until she felt sick.

Anna pushed the hair from her eyes and straightened her back. Her knees ached and her head hurt. It felt like hours she'd been in her garden, weeding the roses, and wondering why.

For two days she'd wondered if León had taken the sun away with him. Even when it emerged this morning, the world was no brighter, although its late afternoon heat now burned through her clothing. Nothing seemed real. She was hollow, a shell of her former self.

She pulled at another weed, but her motions were wooden, futile. Why had they once seemed important?

A voice startled her. "I had to come. I'll do whatever you say, Anna. Just let me see you."

Anna's pulse raced. She looked over her shoulder. León stood in the gate, a few feet behind her. His eyes were bloodshot and his skin sagged from the bones of his handsome face.

"León, oh, León." The weeds she'd gathered spilled from her apron as she ran to him. He gathered her into his arms and carried her into the house.

In days that followed, a shadow hung over the stolen interludes. They were thrilling, but at the same time, less than satisfactory. Anna longed for something—something she thought would reveal itself, but never did. If León felt the same, he didn't show it. All constraint had fallen away and he seemed to revel in her company. He'd never been happier, he said.

A vise locked around Anna's chest. She tried to pray, but words would not form. A cloud hung between her face and God's. This was sin. It had a wicked name. She could not go on.

After two weeks she found her voice. "León, we must stop this. It's wrong on every level. God forbids it. Juliana befriended me when I needed it most. She'll find out and be hurt."

"You're worrying about Juliana? She doesn't care about either of us. No one but herself. If you leave me, I'll have no reason to live." Tears stood in his beautiful eyes.

He pulled her into his arms and kissed her. Anna's fears melted. Her reasons the trysts must end felt trite and stale, even absurd. She loved him. He needed her. It had to be enough.

In a matter of two months' time, Anna's dilemma was no longer hers alone. A baby was on the way. She'd known it was a possibility, but she'd hidden from any thought that it might happen. Her mind reeled with the thoughts of consequences. It was now reality—a reality in which she and León would be revealed to Juliana, to Ramona and Antonio, to Fray Serra, and all of Monterey society as faithless liars.

The thought of Ramona and Antonio having to bear pain that was rightfully hers made her nauseated. They had believed in her.

Fray Serra couldn't allow her to teach in the mission schoolroom in her condition. The padre's loving concern had strengthened her from the beginning. He'd warned her of the dangers, counseled her in remaining true to God's commands. If only she'd heeded him.

She'd been taught to prize God's truth. It was her protection in an uncertain world. How could she have allowed physical thrills to lead her away? Guilt weighted her shoulders as if she bore the heaviest of burdens. Her body ached and trembled.

The sour taste in her mouth had nothing to do with the pregnancy's morning sickness. She cradled her stomach and rocked back and forth, imagining the tiny life within. A pang of regret stabbed her. Her baby would never know the security of a Christian father's devotion as she had. Her child would not have the wisdom and care of a father who loved God first and learned from Him how to love his wife and family. A woman and her illegitimate child faced ostracism from the church and from society. Her sin would harm her baby.

She wrapped her arms tightly about her body and whispered, "I'll protect you, precious one. You'll know every day how much your mother loves you." But would it be enough?

She couldn't imagine what León would say. An unplanned child could not be welcome news. Would he send her away before the *embarazo* became visible? Where would she go?

Fourteen

Anna finally found the courage to tell León. Tears rolled down her cheeks and her body shook. She stole a glance at his face, and a jolt shot through her. His expression was ecstatic!

"*¡Mi encantada!* A child born of our love! Why the tears? Did you imagine I'd be upset? *Querida,* this is the happiest moment of my life!"

What was wrong with him? This was not God's plan. A child was on the way, a baby born of stolen hours in the arms of the husband of her one-time friend. She had betrayed Juliana's trust; but far worse, she'd betrayed her faith.

Anna's chest burned as she thought of the moment when her sin would be revealed. How would she bear it?

León's face glowed. He kissed along her throat. "Oh, Anna—"

She pushed him away. He should be entertaining at least a few doubts. Sharing her sense of shame. Her voice was sharp.

"How can we tell Juliana? She'll be so bitter. I'll bear your child when she cannot. No!" Anna covered her face. "How could I have allowed this to happen?"

León took both her hands, pulled her close, and kissed her forehead. "Don't blame yourself. I wouldn't be denied. I want you as I've never wanted a woman. You understand me in ways I've never been received. Your love has restored me."

Her fears began to drown in the deep pools of León's amazing eyes. Spellbinding, worshipful. He had never appeared more beautiful.

"Trust me, *preciosa*. I'll take care of everything. I'll find the right words for Juliana. What we have isn't wrong. The baby is proof of our joy. You mustn't feel ashamed of our love."

His long fingers rubbed her cheek and his dark lashes sparkled. Tears! Perhaps he was right. Juliana had cast him out. A husband didn't deserve such treatment. He'd tried hard. They both had.

"Juliana will see the baby as a blessing. You of all people must know how she wants one. She was willing to take an Indian child from the mission, but we can offer her one of de Montaraz blood. She'll listen to reason. She could not expect me to give up my manhood to her cold withdrawal."

Discern the meaning beneath the words. For a moment Anna felt Fray Serra standing beside her. Her legs turned to jelly.

A child of de Montaraz blood? Juliana's accusation about León's pride in his bloodlines echoed in her head. *Cold withdrawal?* Was he punishing his wife by turning to her?

She took a step backward and stared at him.

What had she unleashed? God's Word did not forbid what was good. There could be no joy for any of them: Juliana, León, her, or the child of this dalliance. It would bring only pain.

León talked on, unaware. "Our son will have the love of two mothers. You'll be at hand to attend him and spend as much time with him as you wish. No child will ever be more loved or better received. He'll have everything he desires and so will you." He kissed her wrist and tried to push up her sleeve.

Anna pulled her arm away and rubbed at the spot his lips had touched. She strained to hear his words above the roaring in her ears.

"I'll adopt him so he can legitimately bear the name of de Montaraz. He'll inherit an empire."

Her world turned upside down. What a fool she'd been! Anna pushed free of his arms and fled out of the cottage. She ran sobbing to the corrals, León on her heels.

"Anna, have you gone mad? This should be the happiest moment of your life. Come back to the house with me."

She refused help in saddling Consuelo. He pleaded, but he didn't try to stop her from leaving.

"Where are you going?"

"Away from you." She mounted and galloped from the corral, but he followed. The mare was no match for León's big Andalusian. As she headed toward the house, he pulled up alongside and plucked her from the saddle. Consuelo followed behind, stirrups flapping.

Anna struggled, but he held her against his booted leg with one strong arm. All she could picture was the man of her dreams, who would sweep her up onto his black horse and carry her away. Reality was far more painful. León's arm around her rib cage felt like a band of steel.

"You're hurting me! I can't breathe." He reined up under a spreading oak and allowed Anna to slide to the ground. He leaped off and reached for her arm.

"Don't touch me." Tears streamed down her face. She held up her hands and backed away until she was against the tree. His hands on either side trapped her as she tried to duck beneath his arm.

"Look at me." He caught her chin. Inches away, his breath was moist and warm against her cheek. "Stop this foolishness! It's natural for you to be emotional in your state, but this turmoil cannot be good for the baby."

"Let me go!"

"Not until you listen to reason."

She stopped struggling and stared up at him. "Reason? Oh, I had reason, León. I wanted your love enough to turn my back on the teachings of a lifetime. To go against God's command that a relationship between a man and woman belongs to Him. I traded the security of years of God's wisdom and protection for fleeting moments in your arms."

"Not moments. You have my love and my promise to take care of you and the baby forever. What we have was meant to be."

"What we *had* was not love." He winced at her stress of the past tense and tried to speak. She placed her fingers against his lips. He tried to hold them there for a kiss, but she jerked free.

"You were patient and clever. I see that now."

He froze. "What do you mean?"

128

Anna struggled against tears. "Did you manipulate Juliana as you did me? Were all the flowery phrases she despised designed for me? You knew how I admired my scholarly father. How I searched for a man to compare."

"*Querida*, what are you talking about? All I knew from the start was that my love for you is real."

"Your *desire*, León. You never loved me. Fray Serra warned me how easy it is to lose God's path in the midst of wealth and sophistication."

"You're speaking nonsense, Anna." León reached for her hand, but she curled it into a fist.

"You want a son and Juliana cannot give you one. I had the proper bloodlines so you made a child with me. Was this your reason for hiring me? You mean to give my baby to Juliana and earn her forgiveness. She'll never allow me to hold my own child."

He shook his head. "None of that is true. I couldn't stop myself from falling in love with you."

"I know real love. I saw it between my parents. It's steadfast, no matter how difficult circumstances become. It honors vows to God and to the other. You couldn't have betrayed Juliana if you understood. And yet I fell into your waiting arms willingly." Her voice strengthened. "I must do what I should have done long ago. I'm leaving. I will go to Fray Serra."

She tried to pull away, but León took her face between his hands. His beloved features hardened and the magic eyes grew cold.

"Understand this. There is no way I can allow you to leave me. I will care for you and the baby. You'll both want for nothing. If you won't think of yourself, do what is best for the infant. I'll see you tonight."

Anna stood watching him ride to the top of the hill. He paused and stared down at her. Erect on the magnificent animal, he reminded her of a prince surveying his realm. She felt a sudden chill. León de Montaraz was a determined, charismatic man, who wielded great power in the province. How far would he go to hold onto a child to would inherit his empire?

Anna fell to her hands and knees. "Holy Father, I have sinned against You and people around me. Please take all my fears and desires. I give them all to You. Into Your hands."

She stood and raised her head. Nothing moved around her, not even a leaf. Light poured from above, silhouetting every limb, twig, and leaf of the oak tree. It was enormous, rooted deeply in the elements that sustained it. A soft mist seemed to envelop her. *Root yourself in Me. Not in what you think you must have.*

She rose and rode straight to the *casa grande.* A gardener looked up in surprise and grabbed for the mare as she dismounted on the run.

Anna's legs gave way just inside the kitchen door. "Ramona," she cried, and sank to the floor. The tile felt cool to her overheated face, but the smell of strong lye soap from Ramona's immaculate floor made her stomach queasy. All she could see was a circle of feet.

When she awoke, Ramona's concerned face hung over her like a moon. Anna was in Ramona's big bed, not the small one she'd used during her earlier stay. A soft, dampened cloth found her heated forehead. Ramona pulled up a chair, and took her hand.

"Tell me. I can guess at some of the story, but I want to hear it from you."

Anna's voice sounded weak and flat. Her head ached and she wondered if she made sense, but Ramona seemed to understand.

"You must eat. You'll need strength to finish this day." She brought a slab of buttered bread and a bowl of broth. "*Con pan, problemos son menos.*"

With bread, troubles are fewer. How Anna wished the saying were true. Propped by several fluffy pillows, she drank the broth and had almost finished the bread before Ramona spoke again.

"Don León de Montaraz is not the man to rear your child. I have loved that man all his life, but I understand his weaknesses. The child belongs to God."

"I must leave before he finds me. He said he'd never let me go." Anna detested her reedy voice. Her baby needed her to be strong. León was determined to hold onto his heir.

"Rest, Anna. Let me pray and think." After a few minutes Ramona lifted her head. "I'll send Antonio to Fray Serra."

"I didn't know he had returned from the mission trip León mentioned."

Ramona's eyebrows rose. "So far as I know he has not been away. Fray Serra will know how to handle León de Montaraz. That little servant of God will speak truth in this matter—you'll see."

Her brow furrowed. "Antonio has been worried about you. He questions me every time he sees me. This will destroy what he feels for Don León—and rightfully so. As your employer, he should have been your protector."

"It was no more his fault than mine, Ramona. I wanted it to happen."

"But it wouldn't have if Don León had not persisted. Men have needs. Women want love."

"It's true I'd never have forced a liaison, but my sin is no less."

"You were attracted to the wrong man. Antonio has been in love with you for some time. He'll be hurt by your choice, but he'll work to help you."

Anna turned her face into the pillow. She didn't deserve anyone's love. How could she face Antonio?

Ramona went to the door and called to the gardener, "Find Antonio and bring him to me. *Muy pronto.*"

Two hours later León strode into Ramona's kitchen. Anna replaced the glass of milk she'd been forcing down. He knelt beside her. Without taking his eyes from her face, he said to Ramona, "Go back to work. I'll take care of Anna. She's not well." Ramona did not move.

Anna pushed away from the table and evaded his outstretched hand. "I'm going with her, León. Fray Serra is on his way. You cannot stop me."

"Antonio told me. There was no need. We could have worked out our differences." The color had bleached from his eyes. A frown seemed permanently etched on his face. "Have it your way for now. I'll wait in my office. Fray Serra will listen to reason if you will not. We need a voice you trust to speak sense to you."

His mouth wore brackets of pain—or anger?—but his eyes beneath his drawn brows eyes were soft and concerned. "Don't hate me, Anna. I want what's best for you and the baby. You must know how much I care for you."

She watched him move hesitantly toward the door. He stopped and stared back at her. Something in Anna wanted to call to him, but she forced herself to turn away. He left without another word.

Her stomach twisted as she poked at an egg growing cold on her plate. "I'll make it up to you another time, sweet baby. Mamá can't face that egg," she whispered.

"Eat something." Ramona rolled a slice of ham into a tortilla and held it out. "For the *bebe*. I must return to work. Wait here."

Anna managed to eat a little in the minutes before Antonio arrived. He took her arm, but he didn't meet her eyes. They walked toward León's office.

Antonio must be beyond disappointed. They'd talked often about the importance of faith and obedience.

Her willful disobedience had hurt him. Her sin had come between Antonio and his friend and employer. Anna was nauseated. With each step her feet grew heavier. Without Antonio's strong arm, she might collapse again before they reached Don León's new office on the front of an impossibly large house.

What would Fray Serra say in the face of this calamity? He might well agree that Don León should rear the child. What could she offer? Certainly no wisdom, and she did want stability for the baby.

León and Juliana could offer him the world, but Anna wanted more. She wanted the steadfastness of a father like hers. One filled with God's wisdom.

Fifteen

Antonio pushed open the heavy doors and led Anna into the room. He remained near, hand beneath her arm, anchoring her to reality. Otherwise she might have thought she was in a dream—or a nightmare.

León sat behind his desk, clenching his fingers together then spreading them with force. He looked up at her and the graceful line of his mouth tightened. Turning away, he found a silver letter knife to finger.

Tension saturated the atmosphere and made the large room feel small. Fray Serra maintained a dignified silence near the door. What had passed between them? Had they already reached an agreement that the baby should remain in secure surroundings? The weight of that thought made Anna's knees tremble. Neither man's face offered a clue.

León's was wiped clean of emotion, but his eyes were wary. A slight ridge between his brows hinted at his feelings. He must want the issue resolved quickly—a path cleared for his claim on a rightful heir—the child of de Montaraz blood that had obsessed him for years.

The friar took her hand. "Anna, my dear." Fray Serra's expression displayed his customary serenity, making her chest tighten. He must be so disappointed in her. How could he now believe she would be a fitting mother to a child?

The padre looked much older than when she had last seen him. He had lost weight and his shoulders bent forward, making him appear smaller than ever. She fought tears when he placed his hand on her shoulder.

"Come with me to the garden. I will hear your confession." He caught an audible breath and rubbed at his chest.

León half rose from his chair, but Fray Serra stopped him with a motion. "Confession is a private matter, Don León. I will hear yours when you are ready."

Anna thought the momentary expression on León's face would remain in her mind forever. He looked like a schoolboy caught in a naughty prank. Then his brow furrowed and he growled at Antonio, "Go back to work. I'll deal with you later."

Antonio bristled and did not move. As she walked past, he nodded, a soft expression in his eyes. "Courage, Anna." She struggled to maintain control.

Outside two armed vaqueros guarded the door. A *soldada de cuero,* one of the so-called leather soldiers from the garrison, towered over them, a giant of a man with a large sword at his side. He removed his leather helmet and bowed to the friar as he passed. "I am here for you, Father. Whatever you need."

The friar nodded and murmured a blessing. In the garden Anna knelt in a trance, Fray Serra's hand on her head.

"Don't be afraid, my child. Do you think I have come to censure you? One sinner does not judge another. It is my privilege to help you seek God's forgiveness. His grace is sufficient. Always sufficient."

"But my sin hurt so many. Juliana most of all."

"God is much bigger than any hurt. He loves Juliana, too. And Don León."

Anna shuddered with the need to unburden herself. For almost an hour, she poured out her heart, but she could remember none of her words by the time they reached León's office again. Her legs no longer trembled. The decision was made. She returned with the knowledge that her choice had the potential to alter the course of everyone's life in that room.

Antonio remained in the same spot as before, his face stony; León stood opposite, his arms crossed. He turned his scowl on Anna, but before he could speak, Fray Serra said, "God's command will prevail here, Don León. You have a wife. Antonio and Anna will wed and rear the child in God's precepts. Your name will never be mentioned to their son or daughter."

León roared, "You cannot do this! Anna belongs with me. I am the father of the child." He bellowed for his *vaqueros* and jabbed a thumb toward Antonio. "Take him."

The voice of command cut through the air. Fray Serra pointed a finger at León. "Marriage is a sacred union in the eyes of the church—a sacrament. I speak with the authority of the Holy Catholic Church and the military might of the Spanish Empire behind me. Your influence in Anna's life is at an end. She will find new purpose in God's plan. I pray you will, also. Your God awaits you, Don León."

Marriage is a sacred union. The words crushed Anna anew. Her hand trembled as she touched León's arm, but she kept her voice steady. "I regret the harm I've caused you and Juliana. I stand condemned by my sin." His eyes met hers and the pain in their depths took away her breath.

Somewhere she found the strength to continue. "Fray Serra assures me I'm forgiven by God's Word. I pray that for you, too, León. That you'll find forgiveness and can restore your marriage. You and Juliana need each other."

He jerked his arm away. "You'll regret this for the rest of your life. You could have had everything."

Antonio took her hand and they walked out in silence behind Fray Serra.

Two days later Anna and Antonio entered the chapel of Mission San Carlos de Borromeo. Could she do this? Come to Antonio as a fallen woman with the child of another man growing in her womb? He was her friend, but could she ask him for such weighty sacrifices?

He'd given up the life he said he was meant to lead—the ranges, the comfortable house, the immense herds of wild cattle, and the beautiful vistas of Hacienda de Montaraz, where he wanted to live for the rest of his life. Then there was a child he hadn't fathered. Was it too much?

Anna had another concern, too. One she would not share with Antonio. Wherever she went, whatever she did, it remained at the edge of her waking mind, waiting to spring forward if she relaxed her guard.

Would León really give up his heir without a legal battle? The Governor of Monterey—no friend of Fray Serra's—listened when Don León de Montaraz spoke. The two sometimes met in León's *oficina*. Juliana had scoffed at them. "Cigar smoke and lofty visions. They dream of owning all of California."

Fray Serra awaited Anna and Antonio at the altar. Behind him soared the friars' treasured stained glass window shipped from a ruined church in Spain. Golden morning light poured through and created a rainbow-like aura encircling him. Anna thought of heaven and the beauty surrounding God. It was a sacred moment.

The friar joined Anna's hand with Antonio's and spoke the solemn words that would unite them forever. Phrases about the duties of a husband and a wife joined in a covenant with God—the same utterances made by León and Juliana years before.

Anna's sin arose like a cloud before her eyes and threatened to destroy her newly-found release. León no longer controlled her life. Her sins had been confessed. God had forgiven. She gripped Antonio's hand harder and felt his response. The cloud subsided, and with it the pain in her chest. She focused on the friar's moving lips, and was able to hear his final words.

"*Amar a Dios siempre.* Love God always. Never look back." The friar's gentle eyes blessed the newlyweds. He beckoned them nearer, his voice almost a whisper as he spoke a surprising prophecy. "You will remember these words one day and act on them," he concluded. "Now go into your new life, my beloved children-in-Christ."

There was no kiss.

Antonio led her from the chapel to one of the small houses built for *vaqueros*. They stepped onto a porch covered by a thatched roof and he opened the door.

"Our home. I'll act as *caporal* for the mission herds now. Look around, Anna. No luxury. In time, perhaps I can do better, but don't expect very much. I will add two bedrooms when I find time. That should be enough. If the friars choose to dwell in poverty with their charges, how can we live above them?"

The whole house was not as large as the bedroom Anna used at Casa de Montaraz. She ran her hand along the smooth surface of the hand-hewn table. Atop it a small vase of fresh wildflowers brightened the space. Every surface was immaculate. A bed big enough for two dominated one corner. Its posts were of cedar, with the bark stripped to show the beauty of the knotty wood.

"I made the furniture," Antonio said. "I couldn't bring everything, since my house was bigger. The chest in the corner holds some of your things. Yesterday Ramona helped me pick out what she thought you'd need. I'll retrieve anything else you want."

His face blurred with tears threatening to spill. "It's beautiful. All we need. And the flowers are a lovely welcome."

She faced him. "Can you be happy here with me, knowing what you know?"

And what about me? She was grateful. He'd rescued her and the baby; but was it enough? Anna struggled against a tide of memories. Sweet moments with León—and passionate ones. Could she feel for Antonio the kind of love she'd felt for León?

Antonio's dark gaze searched all the way to her soul. She closed her eyes, unable to bear the scrutiny.

He whispered, "*Soy contento.*"

"You're content now, but can you forgive me? You sacrificed so much. You said you wanted to die on the ranch you loved."

She couldn't bring herself to mention León's name. She didn't want him intruding into their new life. "I gave myself, knowing it was wrong. I'm weak, Antonio. Unworthy of your love."

She turned her back again and touched the silky petal of a poppy Antonio had picked for her. Her chin trembled.

His strong arms encircled her from behind. "Never say that again. You trusted your heart, *querida.* You're a fine young woman, deceived by a man who loved you carelessly." He turned her to face him.

"Oh, Antonio, I've made such a muddle of my life and yours." Tears finally fell.

His gentle thumbs wiped them away. "What you need is time. Time to heal and plan for our baby. I'll give you that, Anna. Press you for nothing. Do you understand what I'm saying?"

"But what if I never love you?"

"Can you respect me?"

"Oh, yes. You are worthy of anyone's respect."

"Then, we have no problem. Nowhere in God's Word does it say a wife must love her husband. A wife is to respect her mate. The husband is the one commanded to love as Christ loves the church." His soft brown gaze caressed her face.

"I can be a good wife, Antonio, and a good mother."

"We'll build a future for our child." He gathered Anna into his arms, her head to his chest, and whispered, "One day, no matter how long it takes, I'll love you into loving me. Until then I'll cherish our child as I cherish you."

The steady thrum of his heart unleashed her tears again. She willed them to stop. She had to be strong for Antonio and the baby.

Into Your hands, Holy Father. Please keep our child safe from León and his powerful friends.

Sixteen

In early August, Fray Serra summoned Father Francisco Palóu from service at another mission. Anna and Antonio joined Fray Serra to greet the priest when he arrived mid-afternoon two days later. At Fray Serra's insistence, they stood on the porch of the friar's small hut. He'd refused to remain in bed, although he struggled for breath.

"Learned doctors say my heart is failing, Francisco."

"Your heart will never fail your people. But I will be honored to serve beside you once again."

"Our native children need us more urgently than ever. Greedy men seek to destroy all we've worked for—take the land for their own, despite promises to our converts that it will soon be theirs."

Anna waited on the porch as Father Palóu, Antonio, and the *Comandante* of the garrison settled the ailing old man back into his bed. Anna followed to the doorway and handed Antonio a basket of fresh bread and a container of beef broth she'd brought with her.

"He must take all the soup and as much bread as you can persuade him to eat, Antonio. He's had almost nothing today."

Anna sat in one of the chairs, remembering the evening with Fray Serra before she went to Hacienda de Montaraz. An inexperienced girl filled with foolish ideas about the life she believed she must have. A large ranch house and a husband of consequence. She had tried so hard to make that dream come true, only to find heartbreak and disillusionment. Far better the life God had planned for her. He had led her to Antonio and the possibility of true fulfillment.

Father Palóu and the *Comandante* came out and took the remaining chairs, talking with Anna while Antonio spooned broth to the friar.

"He'll soon be well again." Palóu said. "I heard him earlier with his converts. A sick man could not sing with such fervor."

The fort commander shook his head. "There is no basis for hope, Father. This saintly friar is always well when it comes to praying and singing, but he is nearly finished."

Within two days, Fray Serra asked for *Viaticum*, the Holy Communion received at the hour of death. "If I can go to the Lord, there is no reason why the Lord should come to me," he said when Fray Palóu suggested he remain in his hut for the service.

Anna held onto Antonio's arm and watched the friar struggle to the sanctuary in worn sandals, loosened to accommodate his swollen feet. Propped by the *comandante* and a soldier, he made his painful way.

Word had spread among the *indios* and they came in crowds, many in tears. The lump in Anna's throat would not allow her to sing with Fray Serra in the *Tantum Ergo* of the Blessed Sacrament, but his voice rang out above the others.

Anna and Antonio waited as the aging Alcantarine remained kneeling at the altar for some time. When he arose to return to his hut, the whole assembly accompanied him. Fray Serra sat on the floor, leaning against the knees of his converts, listening to the Word of God read by Father Palóu.

Anna studied the small room that contained the friar's accumulation of a lifetime of labor: a board cot, a single blanket, a wooden table and chair, a small chest, a candlestick, and a gourd dipper. She whispered to Antonio, "He lived so poorly. Our own small cabin is much better furnished."

"He invested in people, rather than things. His mansion is in heaven."

Fray Palóu spoke to the weeping crowd. "Blessed Father Junípero Serra has remained true to his Franciscan vows of poverty for fifty-four years, the last fifteen of which in California were the most exacting."

Anna smothered a sob. "He won't live to see the birth of the baby, Antonio."

"He lived to see the rightness of his decision to marry us. He gave me instruction on what kind of father I shall be, and what kind of husband to you, *mí amor*. His prayers will be heard even louder in heaven."

Friar Junípero Serra died on August 28, 1784, little more than a month after Anna's wedding. She wept as she had at the death of her father. Bells tolled to announce his passing and hundreds of native people filed past the open coffin, trying to glimpse their beloved *padre* for the last time. On the day after his death, Fray

Junípero Serra was buried within the altar rails of the church.

"The Spaniards are giving him a grand funeral," Antonio said. The cannon of a supply ship anchored in the bay fired every half hour, and guns of the presidio responded. "They're conscious of what all California owed this one man."

Anna nodded. "An impressive ceremony for a humble little man."

"*Sí, mi amor,* but I believe I'm more impressed by the crying and wailing of the *indios,* who almost drowned out the singing of the Office for the Dead. The native sons and daughters lament the death of their father who left his own parents to come to this distant place. His sole purpose was to make them his spiritual family. The lost and the least."

"A father to many. He would have appreciated your tribute. The *indios* were his passion."

"God was his passion, *querida.* He achieved holiness, a life set apart for God. Fray Serra said of himself that his was an ordinary life transformed by the presence and activity of God's Holy Spirit. God will continue to use these humble Franciscans." Antonio shook his head. "If only the governors shared their dedication to native peoples."

Two months later, Antonio burst into the house in mid-afternoon. Anna turned and smiled at him. "You almost made me drop this dough! What do you have to tell me?"

"Don León and Juliana arrived at the mission today. Fray Palóu says they adopted three orphaned boys: an eight-year old, a three-year old, and an infant. A high price for Juliana's forgiveness." He studied her face.

Anna's heart skipped a beat. Some nights, she had lain awake, wondering what she would feel when she heard León's name again. She felt only blessed relief. Perhaps he would not pursue gaining control of her child. Pleased that she was able to smile and mean it, she put the dough aside and went to Antonio.

"I'm glad my betrayal didn't destroy their marriage. León will have sons to inherit his empire and Juliana the children she wanted. I pray they will develop wisdom and faith like yours. I hope they can one day forgive me as you have."

"Of course, *querida*. But better yet, God has forgiven you. Man's forgiveness can't restore as His does." His embrace encircled her.

How quickly her heart was mending in the new life with Antonio. She and her baby were safe with him.

"Perhaps in time, Antonio, I can believe in myself again and your trust will be rewarded."

"Why wait? Believe now. We'll both be happier." They laughed together.

Antonio's gift of forgiveness was strengthening. An accomplished fact, it was there for her to accept and move on to other concerns. His sense of humor was almost as healing. *I smile more than I have in years.*

An amazing man. It was time to tell him she loved him. What she had thought might take years had happened in weeks. She wanted Antonio beside her as long as she lived. Anna longed to see the child in Antonio's arms, the only father her baby would ever know. With Antonio, Anna believed it was possible to one day forgive Don León as God had forgiven her. She must work toward forgiveness. There was no other option with God.

Ramona Aurora Antonia Rivera-Arista was born in March 1785. As she lay in her father's arms, her mother thought back to the day Fray Serra married them.

"Do you remember Fray Serra's words at our wedding, Antonio?"

"They are forever etched in my memory, *mi amor*." His eyes twinkled. "And I remember you asking me how he could possibly know and I answered, 'God must have sent him a vision.'"

"Say them, Antonio. Repeat his prophecy."

"The good Fray Serra said, 'I believe you will bear a daughter, Anna. She will be called Aurora, which means *dawn*. Suns set in our lives and darkness prevails for a time, but in God there is always a new day.'"

Anna added, "Then he said, 'Aurora will shine brightly for God because you will set her feet firmly on the right path.' Together we will set her feet on God's paths."

"Together," he said.

Part 2: Red Sky

A Woman Alone

Seventeen

An island off the coast of Monterey, California, 1787

Red Sky had seen it, but not clearly: a dark presence that hovered near the island and made the women cry out in fear. She hesitated to tell her husband. Achak resisted the idea of visions. He would find it hard to believe The People were not safe. They were the only humans on Far Island. Food was plentiful in the season of green leaves, and not even the threat of an icy storm existed. But the dream persisted, long after Red Sky moved into the cozy confines of her little birthing hut.

Four moons ago, the women of Red Sky's tribal family had constructed the little house some distance from the village. A separate space would allow her rest from the daily concerns of life on the island. Here Red Sky could gain strength to birth a healthy baby. The clan was small, and The People awaited her child as an important addition.

Until the babe was born, only Pachu was allowed to live with Red Sky. Three years ago—soon after The

People had paddled their reed kayaks to Far Island—she had lured Pachu away from the wild dog pack that inhabited the woods. But even his comforting presence could not protect her from the vision of something she could not yet name.

Achak still lived in the house the two had shared in the village before her confinement, but he came to her birthing hut each morning with food and news. One warm and windy morning, Achak crawled inside the tiny door of Red Sky's hut.

"Good morning, my beautiful wife."

"Your words are fine ones, but your face is not happy, husband. This morning's news cannot be welcome," she said.

"The women warned me not to tell you." His mouth went down at the corners. "I told them you would see it in one of your visions even if I did not." Achak's gaze was troubled. "Have the dreams been upsetting you again?"

She ducked her head so he could not read her face. Red Sky wanted to send him away without speaking. His words would make real that which disturbed her, but she had to know. As visionary, she was responsible for interpreting truth to her people, whether or not it made her and her husband happy.

"Tell me, Achak. I sense something brings danger, but I cannot see it clearly."

"I hoped you would not be troubled with visions while you carry the babe." Achak shook his head and exhaled a deep breath of frustration. "Perhaps the truth will set your fears at rest." Still he hesitated.

Red Sky twirled her index finger in the air, the signal to speak.

"Ten Aleuts have come from the North on a black boat with red sails. Strange men. But they seem to offer no threat."

"Say more. Help me see why you call them strange."

"Short, heavy men with eyelids that almost cover their eyes. With them are two bearded giants who give orders. Russians, they call themselves. They have come to take the fur of sea otters."

She gasped. "But the otters are sacred, Achak. The otter skins of Far Island are to be worn only by leaders of the clan—my father as chief, the *oss*, and me as visionary."

"It was the *oss* who counseled your father and The People to greet the hunters as friends."

"The words of the shaman earn respect from my father. What did Father say about these men?"

"When we met in council, the *oss* wanted our men to hunt for the strangers. But Sacha Pal said, 'Do not go near them. They have invaded our island, but they will soon be gone and life will go on as before.'"

"The People should listen to my father."

Achak nodded. "We met the hunters as friends, but we refused to help them kill the sacred otters. The Russians were angered, but Sacha Pal stood firm. He said the Aleut hunters must put up their tents at another spring, far from the village. They agreed. The bearded men say they will live on the boat."

"I will sleep on your words, husband. If it is these men who bring the danger I have seen, I will speak to my father."

"But you are to see no man's face except mine until the birth. What will the *oss* say?"

"My father will deal with the *oss*. He knows I would not break *tabú* without strong reason."

At first light the next morning, Achak came with more news.

"The *oss* has demanded payment for each otter killed. After many angry words, the Russians agreed." Achak sat down with her and held out a string of shiny, green beads. "A gift from the Russians."

Red Sky frowned and shook her head, leaving the necklace to dangle from Achak's fingers. "*This* is what they offer in payment?"

"No, there is to be much more. Iron heads for spears, arrows, and fishing hooks. Iron kettles like those of the mission on the mainland."

A gray cloud formed between Red Sky's face and her husband's. His words caused her to clasp her knees tightly together to keep them from trembling. "What did my father say about the demand for payment?"

"He called it blood-stained. He said the gods would be angered. I agreed, but the two other men and all the women of the tribe agreed with the *oss*. They say The People need what the Russians offer."

"Take me to the high point, Achak. I must see for myself what you say is happening."

The way was steep, but with her husband's help, Red Sky struggled to the brush-covered summit at the north end of the island. Achak's hand pulled her upward foothold by foothold. Just before she reached the top, a familiar sensation seized her. It started as a tingling at the nape of her neck, increasing in intensity as it crawled along her hairline and over the crown of her head to her brow. Her scalp felt as if it were afire.

"Help me, Achak. It is near. The fearful object of

my visions. I must see what it is."

Together they peered over the cliff's edge. Red Sky fell back, her hand to her throat. A large black boat strained at its anchor, rocking amid white-capped waves. Its red prow bore a face carved into a hooked beak, and its red sails were folded like wings on its deck.

"Look at it, Achak! A red-faced bird of prey with a fat black belly. What fills that belly?"

"I see only the Russian's black boat, wife. And there are the hunters." He pointed farther down the beach.

Aleuts' kayaks darted among the otters. The men wore skin shirts and peaked wooden hats that slanted out to shade their eyes from *ismén's* bright face on the water. The kayaks were skin-covered, flat-topped, one-hole craft. They skimmed the water at great speed, and the men used oars with blades at both ends, like those of Rumsen people. The otters were quick, but Red Sky saw one pulled up at the end of a long harpoon. Many others floated on stringers in the wake of each kayak.

"The water is red with the blood of sacred otters. The gods will be angry that Father did not stop the slaughter. He should have done more."

"The *oss* says it is not wrong. The Russians bring gifts to our people and the animals are many. Payment must be made for each otter they take. Kelp beds stretch for a great distance on both sides of the island, filled with otters."

Red Sky thought about his words. The *oss* was a wise man, but her stomach still churned.

She grew suddenly weak and staggered. "My head aches and my skin is cold. Take me home before the seeing sickness comes upon me." Perspiration beaded her brow and her knees threatened to buckle.

Achak's strong arms made the labored descent possible. In a trot he carried her through the scrub as darkness closed around her. When Red Sky opened her eyes, they were in the birthing hut.

Bent over her bed, Achak stroked her brow. "Are you free of the seeing sickness, wife? You said many strange things."

"The dream is still with me. I see the black bird with its red face and great hooked beak. It takes wing and pounces upon many victims, swallowing them. I must speak to my father."

When *ismén* was low in the sky, Red Sky met Sacha Pal outside the door of her hut. The *oss* stood at a distance, a short, wizened man, shaking his feathered stick and muttering incantations to protect the willful woman who would break *tabú*.

Her father stood straight and tall, despite his years. Red Sky had been born late in his life, the child of a second wife after the death of his first. His hair hunt straight and thick, cropped above his shoulders, with not a gray hair visible. His dark eyes were keen and sharp as he studied his daughter.

Sacha Pal's head inclined side to side as he listened to his daughter. He backed away when she reached out to touch his arm, but his voice was gentle.

"There is nothing more I can do, my daughter. The People have spoken. They desire what the Russians offer. I, as their chief, must accept their will."

Achak put his arms around Red Sky. She trembled from head to foot as he led her to her bed. Nothing he said could soothe her. A hard knot remained in her stomach from that day.

❧

Almost three moons passed before Achak said he and the other Rumsen men would gather the next morning at the shore. "The Russians and Aleuts are leaving Far Island. We will see them off and receive payment for the otters. I will come to you when they are gone."

Red Sky did not reply. During the night she offered sacrifices to the gods, pleading with them not to turn their anger on The People because of the slaughtered otters. She would go to the high place. Nothing could keep her from watching the Aleut's departure.

She arose at first light. Although Pachu was with her, the effort to reach the brushy summit of the high place was much more difficult without Achak. The child was heavy within. Toyon bushes scraped at her legs, and whining mosquitoes added their misery. Perspiration burned her eyes and stung the scratches and insect bites.

Ismén traveled far up the sky before she reached the top. No breeze blew. The air hung hot and thick with the smell of the sea. Tension filled her as she crouched behind a large boulder some distance from the cliff's edge.

The large, gray wolf-dog beside her made a rumbling sound in his throat. A crest of hair lined his spine and he stared up at her. She could smell his breath and read the concern in his strange eyes, one amber and the other a mottled blue.

"Silence, Pachu. Do not move."

He settled, head on his paws, but the thick fur

remained ridged on his back.

Crawling on her belly to the rim, Red Sky lay panting with the effort. She pushed forward until she could peer over without making her presence known.

She beckoned. "Come to me."

Pachu crawled as she had, and offered a low rolling sound deep in his chest when he stared down at the scene before him. Strong light bleached the sand white. In the bay, the red-faced bird of prey stirred restlessly on its tether. Five hunters paddled their *iqyax* back and forth to a large flat-bottomed vessel anchored near the sand.

Three other Aleuts stowed bales of otter skins atop each kayak as it returned to the beach. Two more stacked their long bows and hunting weapons near their rolled-up tents. Broad-faced men, their shoulder-length black hair fell over their faces as they worked.

One turned in her direction and a shiver coiled down Red Sky's spine. She held her breath, but he gave no sign that he saw her. Tattoos marked his forehead and cheeks, and a long sliver of bone pierced his nose. An ornament of beads hung from his chin. He was dressed in a skin shirt and loose trousers, and his feet were bare.

The five men of the Rumsen village emerged from the scrub forest. Her father led the procession a short distance out onto the beach. The women waited at the tree line. Sacha-Pal folded his arms and watched as the Aleuts prepared to depart. Achak had said her father and the *oss* would perform a farewell ceremony before they received the promised bounty for each otter skin.

The two bearded Russian giants from the black

boat waited near the shallows. The young one's long, dark hair framed a rugged face outlined by a trimmed black beard. He stood erect, tall boots planted in the sand, and muscled shoulders thrown back, showing him as a man to respect—or to fear.

At his side stood an older, even larger man. A yellow beard sprouted from his face into a bush that covered his cheeks and hung from his chin. His girth was larger than any tree on the island. He called and motioned to the Rumsen men, showing his teeth, as he pointed to a large, painted chest that lay in the sand between them.

Yellow-Beard threw back the chest's lid, but Red Sky could not see its contents. Did it contain the payment the *oss* had demanded?

Sacha-Pal approached the giants, the *oss* at his side. Despite the heat, both wore their otter skin capes for the important occasion. They held up their hands in greeting.

Without a word, the younger Russian drew his curved blade and plunged it into the chest of Red Sky's father. Sacha Pal sank to the sand, his hands clawing the air. The *oss* turned to flee, but Yellow-beard awaited him, long knife glinting in the sun. The *oss* fell not far from her father.

Red Sky groaned. Her heart felt as if it would never beat again, nor could she draw a breath. A white light momentarily faded her surroundings until Pachu jumped to his feet and snarled. He lunged forward, but her arms around his neck held him back. She heard her husband's voice.

"Kill the invaders. Do not leave one standing." Achak and the other men drew their bows. The Russians ran back toward their boat, out of range, while the Aleuts strung their bows. Rumsen arrows felled one Aleut, but his cohorts sent up a cloud of arrows. Achak and the others dropped one by one.

The women fled into the scrub forest, wailing. The Aleuts rushed into the trees and dragged the women, one after another, across the sand, their screams filling the air. Odimas held her baby to her chest. She shrieked, "Do not hurt my son!"

With a growl that carried on the wind, the same Russian who had killed Red Sky's father rushed forward, snatched the infant from her arms, and ran his long knife through the tiny body before throwing it far down the beach. Odimas, face in her hands, would have fallen without the support of the other women.

The murderous Russian collected the otter skin capes of Sacha-pal and the *oss*, and wiped blood from their fur in the sand. He strode in the direction of the wooden boat anchored near the shore, shouting orders over his shoulder.

Red Sky kept her arm around Pachu's neck and spoke softly in his ear. "The People believed that on the farthest island we would be safe from the sickness of the mainland. But something much worse than disease has found us on Far Island."

The dog cocked his head, his strange eyes narrowed in concentration. Ears bent forward, he tilted his head side to the side, as he did when the words were too many.

Two Aleuts stood guard over the women. Yellow-beard sauntered toward them. He grabbed the arms of Odimas and Karroc, the young women of the tribe. They twisted and kicked until he released them and struck Odimas in the face. She fell to her knees as he lifted Karroc high in the air. He shook her violently, and set her on her feet. She followed him, head down, as he walked in the direction of the small craft waiting to take them out to the red-faced bird anchored in the bay.

The black-bearded giant turned to watch the struggle, then trotted over to Odimas. Twisting his hands in her hair, he dragged her to her feet. She clawed at him, but he threw her over his shoulder and waded behind Yellow-Beard toward their boat. The three old women of the tribe had fallen to their knees, moaning.

The hunters returned to their tasks as if nothing had happened. A rising tide washed at the feet of the dead Aleut. When they finished packing, the Aleuts transported the wailing old women with them to the black boat and dragged them aboard, forcing them down into the black belly of the ship. Then two of the men returned to help the Russians row their boatload of furs and the two young women back to the fearsome vessel.

Red Sky watched, trembling and panting for breath. When the red sails raised, she hid her face in Pachu's fur. "You and I can do nothing. It is over. Our men are dead and our women have been stolen. We are alone. Now we must live for the child that grows within me."

Eighteen

Its red wings at last filled and billowing, the black bird pointed its beak toward the North. Red Sky, a hand shielding her eyes, watched it well underway before she ran to her men. Achak was still breathing, but he could not swallow the water she trickled into his mouth. Two arrows protruded from his body, one in his neck and the other near the center of his chest.

"Safe," he whispered and closed his eyes.

He had seen that his wife still carried his child within her. He could carry that blessing with him into the dark Land of the Dead. Red Sky placed her face on his shoulder and lay there for a while.

At last she arose. Her heart was a heavy stone. "No time to grieve, Pachu. Much work lies ahead of us."

Red Sky pulled the arrow from Achak's chest and turned him face down in the sand to protect his face from scavenging gulls. The other two other men had fallen face down, arrows protruding from their backs. Only Achak had faced the enemy until the end.

For much of what remained of the day she toiled, sweating and panting, to drag her father's body into his hut in the village. Achak would have agreed that Sacha Pal should be the first to receive attention. He was the chief of the clan, a revered position.

She filled a large pitch-lined basket with water from the spring bubbling nearby and set it safely aside. Then she untied her front apron of grass and the leather one covering her backside to bathe in the cool water. Pachu leaped in and paddled with her for several minutes. Dressed and refreshed she balanced the water basket atop her head for the return trip. Pachu ran ahead.

Red Sky washed her father and dressed him in his second-best cape. It was made of the wings of cormorants sewed to a sealskin liner. Too bad about the loss of the otter skins, but the glossy feathers of the sea birds glinted blue-black in the light of a dying sun. A fitting garment, after all, for a brave leader of The People. She propped him into a sitting position against one wall, knees tucked under his chin and hands on his cheeks, as was the custom of her people.

She had not cried since she was a young girl, but now tears she could no longer hold back streamed down her cheeks. They were a sign of weakness— useless things that made her head ache and her eyes burn, but she was helpless to stop them.

Her chest ached as if her heart had been torn away, leaving only a bleeding stump. She felt unable to move, to think. How could she manage without her father, her husband, and the rest of her tribal family?

Pachu nuzzled close and licked away the tears. His presence brought her strength. She must survive and birth the baby. Together they would continue the ways of The People. Rumsen women were strong. Red Sky would make them proud.

She and Pachu remained in her father's hut that night, eating goat jerky that women of the tribe had preserved. From her bed at her father's feet, she could not see him, but his presence comforted her. Sleep was impossible. She must think of a better way to transport the other bodies. Restless hours crawled by.

Pachu suddenly uttered a low growl and his hair stood on end. Bushes rustled and a snout poked through the open doorway—one of the wild dogs. Pachu jumped to his feet and bared his fangs in a snarl. The snout disappeared.

"You still rule. They fear you. Come back to my side, brave one. I miss your warmth."

The dogs had been left behind by Esselen tribe, who had inhabited the island until they were evacuated by order of the Gray Robes many moons ago and taken to the mission. Some had been ill with spotting-sickness. After their arrival, the illness killed many of The People, including Red Sky's mother, Dukah. Her father then fled the mainland with the few Rumsens who were willing to go with him. They had rowed from island to island until they reached the one at the edge of the world.

Red Sky arose when faint light tinged the eastern sky. She and Pachu gnawed at another strip of jerky. "It is good that my mother has gone before. She will welcome my father, Achak, and the others to the Land of the Dead."

Pachu nudged her arm. He always knew when she was disturbed.

"You are right. We have much to accomplish. You can help me. I have thought of an easier way to move the others. We must hurry to bring them to their rightful places and perform the ritual that will send them to their peace."

On the beach, Pachu scattered the gulls that surrounded the bodies. Then he chased after sandpipers while Red Sky gathered poles the hunters had used to dry their otter skins. From them, she constructed a sledge. Longer poles formed the two sides. She lashed crosspieces in place with strands of dried black kelp washed up on the beach. Bull kelp was as strong as seal sinew. It also formed the ropes with which to drag the sledge. She stood back, admiring her work. Then she called her companion.

"Work, Pachu, work." She placed one rope in her mouth and tugged to demonstrate what he must do. He took the end of the other kelp cord in his mouth, set his feet and pulled back. Together they were able to move Achak and the other two men in a single day.

That evening Red Sky rummaged in each reed house for fishing hooks, digging sticks, cooking utensils, and other implements. In her own hut, she found the two whalebone needles Achak had made for her. He had worked for hours one stormy afternoon to hone and polish them to perfection, then presented them with pride. She caressed the treasured needles and stuck them into a roll of sinew strips, before tucking the small ball away in the large leather pouch at her waist.

Most importantly, she gathered all the medicinal herbs and powders from the huts of the *oss* and of

Odimas, the woman mid-wife and healer.

"And her bear claw, Pachu. I will need it at the birthing."

Red Sky collected other valuables: her mother's bowl and spoon made from the burl of an ash tree; dried abalones; berries and roots; a few long strips of goat jerky; and a bag of precious sea salt.

A small but important beginning to a winter stockpile—one that would guarantee strength to birth and make milk for the little one. Red Sky cached her smaller treasures in finely woven baskets of her people and set them on her sledge, covering them with hides and furs the Rumsen women had painstakingly tanned.

Gasping at the odor, she dragged each man into the conical hut that had been his home; all except Achak. She placed him next to her father. They would begin the journey at the same time on the single road that led to the Land of the Dead.

She dressed Achak in his finest sealskin cloak. Next to him, she placed his bow. Father's she kept for herself. Both were made of yew trees that grew on the mainland and were strung with sinew, but she found her father's easier to manage.

"It is *tabú* to keep my father's bow, and implements of the other dead. They may decide not to leave their possessions, but I will be happy if their spirits linger. Why should I fear them? They are my family."

The *oss* had warned against such practice, but he was not here to punish her. She needed Father's bow and the other tools to survive.

Red Sky glanced at the *oss's* hut in the sacred stone circle at the village center. There, the shaman had danced for the hunt and made music on his flute. Any prayers for the sick that remained within him would be released with his spirit.

She found her father's arrows in their fox-skin quiver beside the door. Each arrow had three feathers on the end to make it fly straight. The arrowheads were made of stone or bone. Only one had a point of iron from the mission.

"It has never been in flight, Pachu. He kept it to use against an enemy. But it was in his hut when the foe disguised as a friend turned on him."

When all was ready, *ismén* was vanishing from the heavens. Red Sky stood outside each hut and chanted sacred words to release the spirits hovering above the bodies, and send them on their journey. Then she set fire to every house in the village. Later she would collect the bones and conceal them in a cave.

The only structure spared was the prayer house, which stood apart from the others, near the power of the spring's healing waters. The hut's doorway was even lower than that of a dwelling. One had to crawl inside. Both men and women used the prayer house in times of need, whether of the body or of the spirit. Red Sky could not burn the sacred structure. Inside, she could find renewal or the courage for a hunt.

Pachu beside her, she sank to her knees and watched the flames eat away her father's house. On the way to the Land of the Dead, her people would stop to drink water and eat sacred sugar. Then they must travel through thick foam like that cloaking the edges of the sea after a storm. On the other side was the Land of the Dead. It was the belief of The People, but the thought now disturbed Red Sky.

"I heard of another God at the mission, Pachu. He

does not speak of the Land of the Dead. He teaches that people can live with Him forever in a beautiful place. He meets people at the mission inside the house with the crossed sticks on top. There I watched a Gray Robe wash the heads of both Father and Achak. He called them *Cristianos*, followers of the God *Cristo*. Perhaps my father and Achak are alive with Him, instead of in the Land of the Dead."

The thought warmed her. Red Sky wished she had learned more of the God, *Cristo*. But in her short stay at the mission, she had been a young and willful girl who did not always listen to teachings of her elders or of the Gray Robes.

Had she really changed? She was disregarding the teaching of the *oss*, with its many *tabús*. If he was right, she was inviting disaster. She threw her head back and emitted a high-pitched sound, then stamped her right foot three times and waved her hands above her head. The *oss* and her father were now freed of any responsibility for her keeping the weapons and implements of the dead.

"Come, friend Pachu. We must turn our faces away. We have done all we can for the ones we love. It is the last moon before the storms begin."

Pachu barked, as if he remembered the ferocity of frigid winds that swept down from the North.

"We must gather and dry abalones and the little silver fish that provide light for our hut. Many large fish must be smoked on planks beside the fire, and other foods found. We will pull the canoes farther from the water in their secluded cove and repair the smallest one for our craft."

Red Sky scratched the place on his chest that

made Pachu close his eyes. "You will help me move my birthing hut far from this blighted place. I know of a secret spring on the north end of the island. It is hidden by toyon bushes and a fold of the earth. Winter will be long and lonely, but we will survive. We must continue the way of The People."

She speared two fish that evening. They ate in companionable silence at the fire circle outside her birthing hut. *Orpeto-ismén* shone brightly overhead, silvering the forest around them. Flames flickered brightly. A breeze carried the salt of the ocean. A wild dog howled in the distance. Pachu threw back his head and answered, a sound that sent shivers down Red Sky's back.

"You will go to visit your wild tribe soon. I wooed you away from them when you were very young, but you have not forgotten your family. When you answer them, I know it will not be long before you leave me. But you will return before it grows cold. You have learned to enjoy the warmth of a good fire and food you do not have to hunt in icy winds."

Pachu showed his teeth in his dog-smile and trotted to the door. He waited there for her to join him. For the first time, the baby danced within her. She had felt stirrings within her for a moon, but this was different. Much stronger. Red Sky hugged her stomach.

"You dance like a leaf in the wind. I will name you Little Leaf, sweet baby girl. I have seen you in my dreams. I will teach you all I learned from my father and mother. You will grow up strong like me, and we will roam the forest and paddle our canoe on the ocean, taking all that the gods give to us for life. We will continue the ways of the ones who left us."

Pachu barked his impatience. Red Sky entered the hut with him and they sat near the glowing fire.

"You will be happy here on Far Island with your mother, baby girl. No fears. If the Aleuts return on their black bird, Pachu will give us warning, and you and I will remain well hidden. Good night, sweet babe, and our protector, Pachu."

The next day Red Sky dismantled her birth hut and lashed its core ironwood saplings and reed walls to her travois beside the baskets holding the treasures from her village. She gathered her otter-skin cape and the sacred feathered stick the *oss* had given her.

Pachu moved strongly at her side, pulling the load on the trip to the ravine she had found at the north end of the island. Using a large scallop shell, she scooped out a flat place near the spring. Thick bushes surrounded the clearing.

Here she rebuilt her cone-shaped hut and placed woven reed mats inside for her floor. Her food and belongings were secured within. Digging sticks and hunting implements stood ready beside her doorway. She rolled a large round rock near to protect the opening from thieving red foxes, for she knew that Pachu would soon leave her to run with his wild brothers.

Her days would be busy, preparing for life on her own. Far Island offered many food resources, but there would be no men to hunt sea lion bulls or the wild goats that roamed the heights. Bad things were prophesied by the *oss* for women who felled an animal with a bow and arrow. Her breath came faster with the thought.

But the *oss* had counseled her father to make friends with the Aleuts and demanded payment for the otters. Perhaps his wisdom was not perfect. She would attempt to shoot a goat. An arrow dipped in a weak poison made from the skin of a fish would temporarily paralyze it. Its dried flesh would bring much strength to her milk for the baby.

Red Sky slept soundly for several hours, but waked as Pachu's wet tongue licked her cheek. She rose and went to the doorway with him. It was not yet light.

He stopped just outside. Firelight and a moon growing pale turned his eyes into shining slits. Pachu tipped back his head and howled. Then he disappeared into the scrub forest to pad his way toward weeks of adventure with his kind.

She had only borrowed him from the wild pack. As Pachu matured, the call of his kind became stronger. One day he would leave her forever. His wild heart would call him to his other life.

But not yet, Pachu. Little Leaf and I need you.

Red Sky returned to her bed. Without him, she had only the strength of a woman to sustain her through her days of food gathering. The thought gave her little worry. Pachu always seemed to know where she was and a shrill whistle or two brought him to her. He would be there to protect her after the birth of the baby. The thought tightened her chest.

A woman alone to accomplish the bringing of new life. If only the Russians had not come. Because of their greed and cruelty, her father was not here to welcome the babe. There was no Odimas, with her extraordinary medical powers. No Achak beside her, loving, fearless, and capable.

The coming of the baby had proved his manhood to the tribe. When she was certain she carried a child, she had said to him, "Will you be sad if I do not make a son?"

He laughed. "No man could have a stronger help-mate than you. Another like you will make me the envy of all men."

Little Leaf. Achak would have liked the name. Now he would never see his child.

And the women. Shameful for a man to force himself on a woman. Women were to be respected. Wooed the way Achak had done. Not dragged away screaming and wailing.

In the absence of her mother, her tribal sisters would have cared for her during and after the birth. How would she manage without her family on an island that attracted killers of the sacred otters?

One thing she knew. She would plunge her knife into the chest of the next fur hunter who gave her opportunity. It would be expected of her by her tribal family.

Nineteen

P achu had been gone over a full cycle of the moon. The child was a weight within. A strong wind whipped Red Sky's long black hair across her face, lifting grains of sand to torment her eyes—the third day of its bluster. The storm had built steadily and now she struggled against its strength, leaning forward with each heavy step through the sand.

Most worrying was the chilly breath of winter nipping at her senses—the aroma of pine forests, the taste of smoke from campfires in the distant north, and the odor of ice. The people had no word for it, but she recognized the smell. The frozen north sent a reminder in this gale. The next one would be much colder. Time grew short and her cache of food was too small.

"Oh, Achak, I need you," she wailed. Her words flew away on the wind.

Icy squalls would soon keep her huddled near a fire that demanded constant attention. A man could cut and carry much driftwood. Even on the coldest day, he could don his furs. With his brother hunters, he could attack a sea lion in the cave, where it slept with others of its kind. A large kill like that would ensure her survival through other storms on the heels of this one.

Why think of it? It took three men to subdue the beast with nets, and great strength to drive a spear into its heart.

Windy weather conditions had spoiled her hunt on several days. Animals were tricky to find in their shelters. The goats had eluded her, just as they did wild dogs, on the crags they roamed.

From the sea she had fared better. She had collected many *awlún* and dried them. Abalones were abundant, but it took her stick to prize them loose from rocks at the edge of the sea.

The store of acorns The People had brought with them from the mainland to Far Island was long gone. If only she could return to the trees her ancestors planted. They stood in straight rows, their acorns plentiful— easy to gather and grind into flour. The thought of acorn porridge, soup, and bread made her mouth water.

She whistled again without much hope. "Pachu! Pachu!" Many times she had whistled and called for him, but each time the wind snatched away her summons. Her jaw ached from grinding her teeth. She needed his strength.

The beach was her last desperate effort of the day. Red Sky slogged to the edge of a tidal pool beside a boulder. Three sea bass! Longer than her arms, they huddled in the boulder's shadow, trapped by the storm surge and a receding tide. Her hands shook as she lifted the fishing net she carried in a roll on her shoulders, and noted a small hole at its center. Tonight she must mend it with twine she twisted from milkweed fibers.

The fish were too large to net with one throw. She tossed a seashell to disturb the fish and hurled the net, only to have a powerful gust cast it down. The price for her mistake of facing the gale, but it was difficult to think with the constant roar in her ears. On the other side of the pool, sand stung her legs, but at least her eyes were protected.

One by one she netted the bass and dispatched each with a mercy stroke of her fish club from the pouch at her waist. She added each to a twine stringer and prayed for their spirits. Praying helped them to be reborn and assured a future supply.

Scaled and cooked on wooden planks before a hot fire, well salted to preserve them, they would be tasty. Bass were her favorite fish. Half of one would provide the night's meal. A whole one would bring strength for the birth, and the remainder she'd save for the celebration with Pachu after the safe coming of Little Leaf—if Pachu returned. What if he remained with the wild dogs forever?

Red Sky bent her neck to receive the rolled net, stretched it along her shoulders, and maneuvered the heavy string of fish to rest on its thickness. She turned her weary steps toward home, her feet sinking deep into the sand with the load of her catch. Twice she had to stop and rearrange the stringer.

Following the creek to its source, Red Sky reached her campsite—a good choice with its bubbling spring and the sloping sides of the ravine to offer protection from the wind.

Too weary to take another step, she fell to her knees, head to her chest, and rubbed at her belly. "Do not worry little one. Your mother will find food enough to keep us."

A cold muzzle touched her ear. Pachu!

A dead rabbit lay at his feet. He maintained a dignified stance and waited for her greeting. Red Sky put her arms around his neck, and for the second time since the destruction of her family, tears coursed down her cheeks.

Pachu's mismatched eyes questioned her.

"You are right, my friend. Strong women do not cry—not even in joy. My heart leaps to see you. You have brought food. The rabbit will simmer tonight with wild onions and mushrooms for tomorrow's first meal. Tonight we dine on sea bass roasted over the fire."

After a meal of roasted fish, wild carrots, and berries, Red Sky slept for hours, awakening only when Pachu jumped to his feet and growled. The stone did not cover the doorway tonight. There was no need with Pachu beside her. Bushes rustled outside.

"Stay, Pachu. It is probably the dog who has been coming around since you've been away. Do not follow him."

Was it the big black one that had already nosed around her camp three times in Pachu's absence? She had never seen him before the Aleuts left. They must have left him behind.

"I cannot let you risk a fight with him. I need you beside me, strong and ready for the hunt."

Morning dawned clear and bright for the second day since Pachu's return. Red Sky's heart was a feather within her chest. A sense of rightness bubbled inside.

"You brought good fortune with you, Pachu.

Today *ismén* shines as brightly as yesterday when we repaired our hut and made a lighter sledge." It stood behind her on the sand, holding a large basket and a smaller one. "Today the sea is calm and my big basket is almost filled with *awlún*."

Pachu barked and jumped high into the air after a gull diving toward the abalones piled inside. Some of them were as big as his head. Their thick, reddish shells glinted in the sun, a temptation to several other gulls watching from the safety of a nearby boulder.

"Good, Pachu. Keep the thieves away. We will slice up a large one tonight for our dinner. The others we will cut into strips and dry for stews on cold days."

Red Sky waded to another rock. Her fingers searched carefully along its bottom side, her sharpened digging stick in the crook of her arm, ready to pry off the snail in one motion. A clumsy attempt would allow the flat-bottomed abalone to clamp down, making it impossible to loosen, and difficult to remove her stick. If it should clamp down on her fingers, it could trap her there in a rising tide.

When the water rose past her waist, Red Sky waded to the beach with a last large abalone. "Come Pachu, we must start for home. On the way, we will fill our other basket with the little silver fish that gather at the mouth of streams. We will dry them with the abalones. They will burn brightly in the dark days of winter."

The morning after preserving their food, Red Sky and Pachu scaled the cliffs of the steep ridge that formed the spine of Far Island's mid-section. The new sledge awaited its hoped-for cargo. The dog's strong back provided a step. She found the first handhold above her and gained the ledge. Pachu scrambled for footholds as she pulled him up beside her.

After they reached the safety of the top, fortune again smiled. Her hand shading her eyes, Red Sky looked around. Not a sail in sight.

This had once been a favored spot for Red Sky and Achak. They often climbed the boulder at the top and stood there, surrounded by space and sea, speculating about what was out beyond the edge of the world. If they could paddle there, would they fall into nothingness?

Now she seldom climbed the high place at the north end of the island to scan the sea. Not after what had happened on the sands below.

Ismén was not yet overhead when Pachu drove a wild goat from the toyon bushes. Her arrow's aim was true. She swiftly skinned the animal, cut it into quarters, and stowed it in her hunting net. She slung the precious meat-filled net over her shoulder and the two began the descent.

They stopped on the first ledge on the way down to eat their fill of berries from vines clinging to the cliff. "We will return, Pachu, for more of these."

The struggle was made even more precarious by the heavy sack. Red Sky had to drop the net onto the last ledge before she inched down.

Above her a loud snarl erupted and Pachu launched himself over her head, landing on his feet below. He dropped into a crouch, growling and snapping his teeth, as he closed the distance between him and a solitary foe.

178

Facing him was the black dog left by the Aleuts. In daylight he appeared to be pure wolf. His narrowed amber eyes were trained on Pachu as the beasts circled each other, showing their fangs. The wolf looked older than Pachu's three years. He might not be as heavy, and perhaps not faster or stronger, but he would have more battle experience: how to harry, hamstring, and trip an opponent. He would have killed before.

Before Red Sky could draw her bow, Pachu rushed the cur in a blood run, seeking to knock the enemy off his feet and onto his back to tear his throat out. But the black wolf dodged the worst of the impact. Then they closed, snarling and clawing at each other, jaws snapping.

Her weapon was useless. An arrow could strike Pachu as readily as it could the wolf. Red Sky dropped to the ground with the precious net of goat meat. The only way she could help Pachu now was to hurry to her hut and bring her lance.

Leaving the sledge, she rushed to her campsite, the sounds of the fight echoing in her ears. It was not far, but she was panting as she dropped her filled net into the safe hole and pushed its heavy rock lid in place. Her hands shook. She grabbed her lance, her club, and a fox-skin bag filled with powdered Yerba Mansa stems and leaves. She sped back to the now-silent battle site.

Both warriors lay on the ground unmoving. Pachu's eyes were closed. Did his heart still beat? Red Sky knelt beside him and laid her hand on his ribs. The faint lift of his side gave her hope. He was breathing.

Before she could examine his injuries, the Aleut wolf lifted his head, growled, and bared his fangs. Jumping to her feet, she stood over him and raised her lance, then lowered it. His throat was torn open. He snarled once more before he dropped his head and closed his eyes.

"Does nothing good come from the Aleuts and their Russian masters? I only wish they lay beside you, slain by my lance. Their life-blood pouring into the soil with yours."

She returned to Pachu. "Look at me," she whispered into his ear. "You must be strong."

He opened his amber eye and his tongue came out. The other eye had a gash above it. Red Sky eased his head into her lap and encouraged him to lap water from her cupped hands before she examined his wounds. A long rip in his belly matted his thick fur with blood. Several deep wounds oozed on his face and the back of his neck. His left front foot was mangled.

She lifted his head and he growled. "I must see, Pachu. Only I can help you."

His throat had two punctures where the wolf's fangs had sought a death grip. She envisioned Pachu on his back, his claws raking his enemy's belly as he struggled to throw off the black Aleut. Which god had protected him?

She parted the hair and sprinkled healing powder onto his belly and neck wounds. He yelped when she massaged some onto his injured foot. "It will ease the pain of the sledge ride home, brave warrior."

Red Sky dragged Pachu's body onto the sledge, causing him another agonized yap. "I know, friend, but you are too heavy for me to lift. I will not allow the sinew lashing to touch your painful wounds. We will go home."

On the way, she kept up a steady flow of words

to comfort him. "I will treat your wounds and feed you meat until you are well once more. We are strong, Pachu. We will be ready to welcome Little Leaf."

If only the feelings inside matched her brave words. Bite wounds often festered and spread their poison throughout the body. She prayed to Coyote, the strongest of gods.

"Three days, Pachu. For three days you have shown few signs of life." She bathed his wounds again, and applied a poultice of yarrow leaves. "You must try to eat."

His head in her lap, Red Sky spooned broth and small pieces of goat meat into his mouth. She massaged his throat, encouraging him to swallow, until he finished the bowl of life-giving stew.

"Sleep. I will wake you soon for more. You must get well. I need you."

Another contraction bent Red Sky over to grasp her ankles. Her back ached almost as strongly as her belly. No longer any doubt. Little Leaf was on her way, even if it was a moon before the expected birth.

She checked her supplies. The backboard held soft rabbit skin to swaddle the baby for the first months of her life. The sacred medicine bundle lay in a deerskin pouch beside Red Sky's bed. It contained herbal remedies and a bear claw. When rubbed on her belly and legs, the claw would give her great strength to push out the baby.

She busied herself brewing two teas she must have. In one gourd bowl she placed crushed fern leaves to help her expel the afterbirth. In the other she crushed the leaves of a bitter weed that would prevent lockjaw, a dreaded aftermath of birthing.

Red Sky stood and straightened her spine. She brought still more driftwood to the pile inside the doorway. The basket of dried silver fish lay near her bed. Four hollowed out stones would act as lamps when she ignited the oily fish.

All was in readiness. She rolled the rock in place to cover the entrance to her hut. Smoke drifted lazily out through the hole in the roof. Her hut was her stronghold. She had done all she could to prepare for the ordeal that lay ahead.

During the last hours of her labor, could she continue the treatment Pachu must have? Little Leaf and Pachu had only her woman's strength to shield them. Would she be able to protect the two beings dearest to her?

Twenty

Early Spring, 1788

Sea captain Gregor MacLeod set his shoulders and gripped the rudder. His fingers were cold on the shaft and a sour taste filled his mouth. He'd misjudged the sea, and it gave no second chances. He should have stayed aboard the *Abagael* until the squall passed, but he'd been impatient. Time was money.

Too late now. His ship was on her way north with her dolphin escort, while he and his crew were left to make the island in an eighteen-footer. The small boat labored in the waves, their island goal hidden behind a rain curtain. Breakers loomed like powerful white horses threatening to breach the bow. Five lives in addition to his were at risk.

"Do or die here, mate! Rough water ahead. Pull hard, then pull harder!" His red-headed Irish first mate relayed MacLeod's orders to four native hunters helping man the oars.

The wind was relentless. Their small craft

struggled among the wave-swept rocks of an island off Monterey Bay. MacLeod watched Sean O'Shea's long legs push against a foot brace and his strong arms strain at the oars. *Skinky-Malinky Longlegs.*

Right now MacLeod wished for his first mate's height. Men of Scottish *Clann Mhic Leóid* were short of stature, but sturdy-built. Strange how he could do one thing and think another, even in a crisis. He'd always been that way. Did what he knew how and trusted God for the outcome. Trust or not, he'd put them all in a hard place with his bad decision.

A sudden lull gave MacLeod time to breathe, but something danced on his spine. The boat was making no headway. The sea was pulling them back. The stern rose. MacLeod glanced over his shoulder and froze. "Rogue wave astern!"

A wall of water loomed behind them. How could they keep the boat from slamming into one of the rocks jutting around them? They couldn't. This could be the one that had his name on it. God's will be done. One of the hunters saw what was coming and crouched as if to jump and swim for it, but his oar mate pulled him down.

"Row! Harder!" MacLeod prayed and pulled till his chest was afire, trying to steady the yawing rudder. The wave swelled, ready to crush them, but the tough little boat rose with it and God's hand pulled them through the sea crags.

MacLeod dragged himself to the narrow beach and motioned toward the boat. "Pull it up oot of harm's way."

When the boat was safe, he and the others dropped to the sand of the narrow beach. His soul shouted praises. "God's miracle we made it. Coulda been it."

When his breathing eased, he struggled to his feet and offered his first mate a hand. "We gotta get at it, Rojo." The nickname was a Spanish word for *red*. "Hope these mission hunters dinna remember enough o' your Irish prose to shock the *padres* when we get back. Fray Peralta will have some verra serious time on his knees."

"Faith, and I'll be saying it was the fault of a sea cap'n who ne'er learned his manners. Easy to believe of a Scotsman who murders the King's English."

MacLeod snorted, proud of his progress in the language. His rough Gaelic burr was as good as O'Shea's Irish sing-song. "Tell that to the barn door, laddie."

"Hafta admit I was beginning to regret me language there for a time, Cap'n. Thinking the Almighty might be dishing out what I deserved." Flat on his back, O'Shea panted, "I'm knackered."

"'Twas the lie God read on yer soul that brought the biggun, mate. Me sainted mither reared her bonnie lad ne'er to curse, and to be ready to die before he'd speak false."

Rojo failed to look chastened. "Mebbe I was thinking of the Frenchies."

"Move yer bahooky, man. We need shelter from this rain. Get our provisions safe before dark. Won't be easy to find dry wood, but now it's April the winter storms are over. Maybe some rain, but we should have mostly bonnie weather for our hunt."

They dragged the eighteen-footer behind the first line of trees, safe from the eyes of Spanish sailors who plied the waters. "Aye, we'll bring it back into play when we rendezvous with the *Abagael* at end o' season."

A dry bed and a hot meal were the order of the day. By nightfall the men had thrown together a lean-to of boughs and found enough dry wood for a fire to cook fish speared by the mission hunters. With a full stomach and the talk of tired men around him, MacLeod rested, content. He didn't need talk.

Could be that was why he'd never found a woman. He grinned, thinking of the one who told him he'd forever keep his face to the wind—navigating, searching. She said he'd never find the right one for him and she could be right. Women talked too much, at least the lasses he knew. They asked questions and expected answers. Silence gave a man time to think and plan.

MacLeod recalled the trip down the coast three years prior, when he'd hunted for a British sea captain who collected furs from northwest coastal hunters. From the deck of his sloop he'd spotted what he thought was a huge flock of sea birds floating on the surf, until the captain said the black shapes were otters feeding in kelp beds near the island. Now he'd returned for the sea otters.

"Och, never regretted buying me own vessel. Sick of the Brits." MacLeod realized he'd voiced the words, so he added, "Risky what we're aboot, mate, but we're set to reap a fortune in black skins. Answer to prayer to find ye at Mission San Carlos." Rojo could play a thick-headed gomerel, but MacLeod was glad to have him alongside.

"Seven years I been there. Learned a few native dialects from mission hunters. Padres paid me to harvest the woods and the waves. Small potatoes to what ye offer, Cap'n."

"Mmmmph," MacLeod grunted the sound Rojo said only a Scot could make. They huddled near a sullen fire coaxed from damp wood, sipping mugs of tea. Maybe this miserable mist would clear by morrow. "By the by, I don't hold with liquor in me camps. If ye brought anything, keep it t'yerself. Want nae blootered hunters to miss their aim."

"Right-o." Rojo poured more tea. "But how will ye pay the natives? I thought ye'd pay in liquor like the Brits do."

"Saw what happened to the natives paid with spirits. Became worthless drunkards. Won't be part of that. I pay in furs."

After a companionable silence, Rojo asked, "How old are ye, Cap'n?"

"Twenty-eight. Ready to return to Skye." He stared into the fire, picturing the rise of the isle's jagged Cuillen ridge and the drop to the gentle white of a soft sand beach. "I aim to show those thieving Brits who took me father's holdings. Might find a bonnie lass, to boot. A body needs a comfortable fortune, before he seeks a woman. A lass needs a life of ease, and sons an inheritance."

He kept his voice nonchalant, but he'd held that dream since a lad, and it became an obsession after his father's death. The man had grieved himself into a grave after his lands were seized and his family expatriated to Nova Scotia. MacLeod's mother died on the voyage and his father by the time MacLeod was fourteen. He'd been on his own ever since.

"Ah'm older by five, but I don't want a woman. Making it fine on me own." Rojo's jaw set.

"Now's the time to make a fortune. Otters willna be here forever," MacLeod said.

Rojo scratched at his red whiskers and growled, "Yah, and neither will we, if the Spaniards find us."

MacLeod shrugged. "Ye can spin a line of blarney and keep us from a rope." He had no real fear of Spanish sailors. He'd been in a firefight or two. "A Rooskie told me of selling otter skins in Canton. Swore Chinese Mandarins pay a hunnerd dollars each. The latest fashion, ye ken."

"Won't keep us warm tonight, Cap'n."

Rojo was right. During the night, wind gusts surged through crevices in the covering branches, and a cold spray spattered the men under their oilskins. There were lulls in the storm and the snoring of his men when MacLeod could hear the steady patter of rain and the brooding moan of the sea.

He heard the occasional howl of what must be dogs left by the natives who'd lived here. He hoped the pack was small. They'd still be a nuisance, thieving around camp or pulling at the furs. He prayed for safety and success.

When morning dawned with clearing fog, MacLeod felt a rush of unaccustomed optimism, thanks be to God. "Hand me another hunk of that fish and let's fall to it."

Rojo swallowed a final bite and drained his cup. "Ye're wanting to try the mission hunters at the baidarkas, right-o? They're skilled in their own reed craft. Should be able to handle the Aleutian kayaks."

"Give 'em time to finish their fish and we'll get to the water. I'm ready." He swelled with pride, thinking of the three small craft he'd purchased.

188

Called *iqyaks* by the Aleutian women who made them, they were lightweight and maneuverable two-man kayaks made of sea lion skin. Using bone needles and a waterproof stitch, the women stretched skins over a frame made of driftwood, bone, and sinew. A forked bow gave a baidarka its unusual stability. In the hands of experienced hunters the craft were almost as quick as the animals they pursued.

The hunters cleaned up the site as MacLeod studied his surroundings. "From the old girl's deck, I judged the island aboot fifteen miles long from stem to stern."

"The ridge above looks to have a few fair-sized trees. Enough to frame a cabin for six to spread their beds, Cap'n, if we don't mind neighbors' smells and snoring."

By evening the men had proved their ability in the baidarkas as well as cut and dragged logs for a cabin. MacLeod chose an inlet about mid-island, protected from the sea by a weathered rim. A nearby creek meandered from the heights and emptied into the cove.

The wild dogs were a threat. Bold and dangerous, they stayed too close for comfort. Couldn't get a count as their shapes skulked and skittered through the trees. He'd offer them a feast of the carcasses, far away from camp. Just one more complication, but God had a few difficulties in His affairs with men, as well. Give thanks, for He is good.

"Perfect site for operations if not for those dogs. How long do ye figure for the cabin, mate?"

"Best plan on six days," Rojo said, "depending if we cut enough timber. Hunters won't work on the

Sabbath. Even when they're not under the padres' eyes, they uphold the commandment. Often wondered how the padres ingrain the habit. Never saw a more strict devotion."

Five days later, the eight-foot cabin stood almost complete and a few thin saplings lay cut and ready to construct drying frames for the skins. As was his habit on the Sabbath, MacLeod scraped his face clean of whiskers, baring his soul while he bared his skin. He dragged up and confessed every sin he remembered committing during the past week. Then he led worship, as close to the Presbyterian service of his youth as he remembered.

Afterwards he and O'Shea set out to explore the island while their hunters rested. The two men made their way to the rock-strewn shore on the southeastern slope. From the cover of an ironwood grove, they stared across an emerald jungle of kelp beds stretching far out into the channel. The feeding ground was alive with otters in their morning forage.

"A model of self-sufficiency, the sea otter."

"Yah, Cap'n, but me high opinion won't get in the way of collecting a pelt."

This would be MacLeod's first try at otters. He'd learned all he could about them. Otters slept at midday in rafts of single-sex groups, wrapping themselves in kelp strands to keep from drifting out to sea. They fed again in the afternoon. Females often floated with pups on their chests during rest periods, and sometimes joined in a third feeding around midnight.

"Verra unlike the silkies I'm used to," he said.

"Totally different from seals. Look at that big'n," whispered Rojo, pointing to a large male floating on his back as he fed on a sea urchin. "Must weigh close to a hunnerd pounds."

To avoid the spines of the urchin, the otter bit through its underside and licked out the soft contents. He used his forepaws to hold his prey and his strong, retractable claws to pry apart the shell as he fed. With those claws he could dine with equal ease on octopus, squid, and fish.

The male otter displayed the dense fur of his kind, the thickest of any animal. He had no blubber in his body to insulate him from icy waters, but his fur coat enabled him to remain warm and dry year round since he didn't shed hairs in seasonal molt. Long, waterproof guard hairs kept short underfur dry. The dense undercoat trapped air to form an insulating layer near the skin. The *pelage*, or body hair, of this one was deep brown with silvery gray speckles, although others in the colony ranged from yellowish or grayish brown to almost black.

"How many?"

Rojo made a quick survey. "Mebbe a thousand in this raft. Probably six or seven hunnerd harvestable. Clever. Swift. No easy prey."

"Aye, the sea otter's a marvel."

Otters were at home in the sea twenty-four hours a day. No need to retreat to a lodge like a beaver, but on stormy days they might seek the shore. Ate, slept, mated, and gave birth in the protection of the ocean, but enjoyed a frolic on the beach now and then. MacLeod admired them. He regretted the day when there would be none left.

"Let's check our possibles. Should be plenty o' forage for one season."

The men made their way down the shore. Schools of fish swarmed the shoals. Edible plants grew profusely. With wooded heights and narrow sandy beaches, they had a good mix for survival. And the island was the most remote in the area, some fifteen miles off the mainland and the fort of Spaniards who'd take a dim view of a Scot harvesting valuable fur. He well might hang with his crew if they found him.

The pessimism engrained in him by his dour, Presbyterian father put him forever at the ready. No use giving in 'til he met the thing that held his name. His blue eyes never stopped searching until they closed at night. Maybe even then one stayed open. He'd been accused.

The two hiked for a time and came upon the remains of a small native village. "Wonder why it was burned? Never housed many people," Rojo said. "The sweat lodge is still in good shape. The padres ordered an evacuation four years ago after disease almost wiped them out."

Rojo built a small fire to brew tea for their noon meal of roasted fish and a few berries. Eyes were on them. A canine snout stuck out and Rojo threw a stick. The gray shape melted back into the brush.

"Morrow should see us finish the frames, and the day after at the hunt, if that suits ye, Cap'n." His eyes narrowed and his jaw jutted. "Too bad we hafta give the padres a cut from these beds." Rojo looked away when MacLeod's gaze speared his.

"None o' that talk, mate. Only fair." Best nip that kind of thinking in the bud. God's way was God's way. "They're losing the labor of four crack hunters. Peralta coulda said nae to me request, or held out for a larger share. Aye, most concerned, he was, that the hunters' families be the ones to profit. He struck a reasonable bargain."

Rojo's voice changed. "'Twas only a jest. Hafta respect Peralta. Works right alongside his converts."

MacLeod stirred his tea. "There'd not be much of good or evil he hasn't seen. Says presidio priests, presidio commanders, and governors have come and gone in his tenure. He stays with the natives. His investments in heaven, he calls 'em."

"I oughta feel a connection with the good padre. The red hair, ye know. Can't trust the fair-haired fellas." Rojo cast a pointed look at his captain's amber locks, shoulder length and matted from sea winds.

"The tawny mane of me ancestress, Helga of the Beautiful Hair, not the cropped red locks of an Irishman."

The laughter was good-natured. They finished their meal and rested, then extinguished the fire and moved up the slopes in quest of meat. The camp had subsisted on fish the skilled natives speared.

"Hungry for something I hafta skin instead of scale," Rojo complained.

"Leave that awhile. Let's look aboot for a place to stash some extra vittles, should a storm force us from camp."

They found a cave that would serve. It was dry and deep enough to shelter six men and their rations. They then returned to the hunt. Within a couple of hours Rojo had his wish in the form of one of the small goats that roamed the heights.

His expression was that of a cat that had supped on milk, if not rich cream. "Wonder any goats left with those dogs," he said.

"God's creatures ha' their ways. He sees to us all. We'll roast the goat underground overnight and savor it tomorrow."

The men hiked along the ridgeline on their return to camp, dropping down from the heights when they recognized the stream that tumbled behind the cabin. MacLeod's blue gaze pierced the forest around him. What else hid in those trees besides wild dogs?

Twenty-One

MacLeod drove his men for two weeks. He worked even harder, always the first up and last to bed, hunting, skinning, treating skins. "Count's up to near a hunnerd-fifty, Rojo, but their rafts dinna show it." He stared out over the multitude of feeding otters. "Though if others take as many, there'll one day be no otter."

Rojo shrugged. "Long since made our fortunes."

The confines of the cabin and smells of camp wore thin. Before sunset, Gregor left the catch for the others to finish the skinning. Time to renew his soul.

The hours hung heavy after a day's work, but he'd brought no books beyond his Bible. He counted heavily on books. They were friends he could trust not to talk when he needed to think, but they could be a distraction when work was in the offing. A man had to stay focused.

MacLeod climbed to the top of the ridge and struck out for the unexplored northern end of the island. After an hour, he heard the strong echo of booming surf.

Scrambling down the slope along a tumbling

stream, he found the creek ended in a drop over the side. He crawled to the edge of a fist of rock and peered down. The whole side of the escarpment had collapsed, exposing an arched underground cavern of immense size.

Gregor slid down the hill for a closer look. After the rocks quit tumbling, he caught a movement in the trees. *Some animal.* He checked his scabbards. His *sgian dubh* was small enough to tuck into his boot, but a formidable weapon. A larger skinning knife hung at his waist. Both at the ready.

He stared upward and his jaw went slack. What God had created here! Lichen-covered rocks glowed in the fire of a setting sun — explosions of orange, red, gold, green, and brown. The stream arched outward, falling in a dazzling spray to join the surf below. Rainbows shimmered in the mist. He felt it in his soul.

"Praise Ye, Father! Praise Ye!"

Surf pounded into the cavern, distant thunder in its depths. He stood frozen, his senses overwhelmed. A sudden cry startled him. Piercing the muted roar of the ocean, it was close by and sounded human.

A panther? Unlikely out here, but they could scream like a woman. MacLeod slipped the slender dagger from the sheath on his boot and pushed it into his belt. He trotted into the trees as the cry became a wail, retreating before him. He paused to pinpoint direction.

Sounds for the world like a bairn, but no wee one could be on the island.

Something padded ahead. MacLeod ran in full pursuit, heedless of branches slapping at his face. He broke into a clearing and held his breath. Leaves stirred in a shrub on the far side. He plowed through the bush and drew up short, unable to believe his eyes. A small woman ran through the woods ahead, cradle board bouncing on her back as a babe bawled. She gave a shrill whistle without missing a step.

Was she calling others? "Hold up!" MacLeod cried.

She was swift, ducking under branches he had to shove away, but the weight she carried gave him advantage. He caught her arm and sized up his catch. Clad in a sea otter skirt and moccasins, the young native woman's upper body was protected only by ropes of shells. More shells woven into her hair sparkled in the dappled light.

No more than twenny-year, if that.

She wrested her arm from his grip and unsheathed a small knife strapped to her waist. She crouched and her black eyes snapped a challenge. Not a fair fight or one he'd have chosen, but she meant business.

MacLeod lunged to grab her knife. She opened a gash in his shirt and drew a little blood. He circled and lunged again. This time he grabbed the arm that held the knife and managed to pin her against him. She held onto the weapon with surprising strength, struggling as the baby wailed. Finally he wrested the knife from her small hand. She kicked like a mule and twisted in his arms until she faced him. Suddenly she went still. She glanced sideways and held out a hand, motioning downward.

Clearly a signal. But to whom or what? MacLeod stared into the bushes, but he could see no threat. No movement of any kind. The only sounds were those of the forest—bird calls and the trickle of a nearby stream.

And the woman's rapid breathing.

"Friend." He said the only native word that came to mind and repeated it. She had stopped struggling, but her eyes told him she was far from finished. His reflection stood in their black depths. A small but worthy adversary. Plenty of men he knew showed less gumption when faced with the sinew and muscle of Gregor MacLeod.

The infant cried harder and Gregor loosed his hold. "Ye need not be scairt of me." He hoped his tone made the words understandable.

She stepped back and whistled again. A gray streak shot from the underbrush. MacLeod shoved her away, knife in each hand, as an animal hurled itself through the air. Gregor braced and threw up his left arm to protect his throat. He managed to stiff-arm the beast with his right and slash with the dirk in his left, opening a gash in the flank.

Wolf or dog? Big and male. He fell, snarling and baring his fangs as he struggled to his feet. MacLeod tensed for another go.

The wolf-dog, far from beaten, stood stiffly, a low growl rolling from his chest. Drawing his head straight from his shoulders, he bared his teeth, staring into MacLeod's face. He took a step forward.

The woman snapped a command and the animal froze, crouched and ready. She held both hands palm forward toward MacLeod and bent to examine the damage to her dog.

Bleeding, but maybe not too bad.

When she stood, the creature rumbled low and threatening, his mismatched eyes trained on Gregor's face. One was amber and the other blue.

Dog, MacLeod decided, but showed wolf heritage in his strength and the shape of his head. Another soft command and the animal settled into a tense, sitting posture. He was still ready for another round.

MacLeod concentrated on soothing the lass. "Friend," he said again. He broke eye contact and sheathed his knives, tucking hers into his waistband. He held out a leather flask of water.

Her breathing slowed, but her dark eyes, visible over the flask's rim, remained wary. Searching his memory, MacLeod recalled the native word he needed. "Others?"

She stared at him for several heartbeats. Her expression turned sad as she shook her head. Her kind had seen many troubles. The bairn bawled louder, not to be denied. The woman unstrapped the board and cradled baby, board and all, against her chest, crooning.

Had she understood him? Alone on this isolated island? He wasn't sure he believed her, but he couldn't take the chance. She'd be safer in camp.

"Tanoch yai—woman here," he commanded as the words came to him. He pointed to his side. A mistake. The dog growled. The young mother bristled and stood her ground until he gestured an offer of food. "Good," he said in English. He'd have to learn her language.

She and the dog stayed beside him on the hike back, and she scorned the hand he offered when the going roughened. At the campsite, MacLeod called, "Rojo! Come oot, man. We hae guests."

Two of the mission Indians stood near, staring and muttering. The others joined them, their faces uneasy. What was wrong?

The dog snarled and his hair stiffened. The

woman looked around and her eyes widened. She edged toward the trees, but MacLeod caught her hand. "Friend," he soothed. "Rojo," he called again.

O'Shea shambled out of the cabin, stretching. "What in the name—? Where'd ye be findin' this young treasure? She's trouble, Cap'n. Mind, her man'll be lookin' and have a quiver of poison arrows. An' I don't like the look of that dog. Yer bleedin'."

"Quit standin' there like a stookie. Talk to her. If I understood her, she's alone. Ran from me, but I convinced her I meant no harm. Bring her some food and get her story."

Rojo headed to the fire and brought a hunk of bread and several pieces of fish, along with a cup of tea. He set the food near her on a large, flat-topped rock at the edge of the campsite and threw a hunk of fish to the dog. "*Ampa,*" he said, stepping back. "Eat."

MacLeod brought water for the animal and laid the woman's small knife on the rock. Her gaze darted to his face. She stood chewing and rejected the tea with an expression of disgust. Och, she was a beauty. MacLeod tried to keep his eyes from going where they shouldn't and glared at O'Shea when he caught him staring. "Ye're a wicked, auld red rascal."

"Sorry, Cap'n, but it's been a while."

When her infant began to whimper, she sat on the rock and nursed her babe. She glanced at the men, but showed no uneasiness. The dog settled at her feet and licked at his wound. It no longer bled.

Rojo sidled over to talk to the hunters. "They don't believe her," he said as he squatted beside MacLeod. "Don't think she's alone. Say the otter skins show she's the wife or daughter of a chieftain. They say others will come lookin'. Their women stick close to family. We need to be ready."

"I found no sign of a camp on the north end. We've seen the rest."

"You seem to think she's tellin' the truth, and she may be, but it won't hurt to have the guns where we can reach 'em, now, will it? My old cap'n used to say, 'God is good, but never dance in a small boat.'"

MacLeod kept eyes on the lass. She cast another peep their way. Rojo was right. She could melt into the woods and bring her men. The young woman intrigued him. He had to learn the rest of her story. Were she and the babe truly alone? What could have happened to her people?

"Aye, I ken her mistrust, Rojo, but she'll have a better chance with us than on her own. How has she kept herself and the bairn fed? Why she's alone is a mystery."

The woman returned the baby to its board. The air chilled and MacLeod sent O'Shea to bring a blanket and one of his shirts. Gregor stood at a distance, demonstrated how the shirt was put on, and held it out. She shook her head. He laid both near her feet and threw another hunk of fish to the wolf-dog.

MacLeod and Rojo squatted a little distance away, mindful of her protector, whose strange eyes never left them. The young woman cast another glance their way, then picked up the blanket and set it next to her. She left the shirt on the ground.

Rojo crept nearer and began talking to her. The dog growled, but she settled him with a word. After some minutes, O'Shea said, "Think I have the bones of her story. Might be true."

"Well?" MacLeod's gaze never left the lass. She was fleet of foot.

"Her name's Red Sky, and her daughter is Little Leaf. The dog is Pachu, whatever that means. She came from the mainland with The People, as she calls her tribe, a couple of years ago—after the evacuation of all the islands."

"I ken ye saying the islands had been cleared of people before we came."

"She said sickness took most of her clan at the mission. Her father, the chief, brought the survivors out here to save 'em from a disease of the Gray Robes. Called it 'the spottin' sickness' and said her mother died of it. Hasta' mean that scourge of the divil himself, smallpox."

Her story was familiar to MacLeod. The story of conquest. Coastal tribes had been decimated by diseases of the Old World. Alcohol and tobacco also proved harmful, as had the introduction of firearms. Some of the tribes had been reduced by two-thirds.

"Red Sky's people rowed their reed rafts from island to island 'til they reached the farthest one, thinkin' here they'd be safe. Thought the hard men would not search the islands again."

"Hard men? Does she mean Spanish soldiers?"

"Right-o, Cap'n. Hard chests and heads that arrows cannot pierce. Their armor, ye know. They hunted down mission Indians who tried to escape."

MacLeod shook his head. "Poor lass. The coming of the Spaniards had to be a shock and a mystery to her people, as the Rooskies and Brits were farther north. Aye, forever changed their world. And who's to say for the better?"

"She said one day a floating house arrived with men who came to hunt the otters. 'Fierce men,' she called 'em. Some were natives with bones in their noses." He shook his head.

"All her men were killed and the women forced to go with the hunters when they sailed. Her husband had built her a hidden hut when she came with child and she managed to avoid the bad men. When she saw our camp, she thought they'd returned."

Rojo took a swig of tea. "Hadda be Russians, Cap'n. Shelikhov and Golikov's men and their Aleutian hunters. I dinna think they'd venture this far south with Spanish ships so often in these waters."

"Other outfits now, but I agree they were Rooskies. Bones in their noses means Aleuts, all right."

"A rough bunch, Cap'n. Kodiak Island's only a jumping off point for them. They're squirmin' to establish settlements as far south as they dare."

He watched Red Sky for a moment. "I'm not surprised she's a bit thin, what with tryin' to make milk for the babe."

"Small and vulnerable, Rojo, but plenty game. God's miracle she made it 'til now."

"Already alone when she gave birth to her daughter. Says she found her dead people, her father and husband among them, and finally moved the bones to a cave. I've seen burial caves. Spooky. They fill the eye sockets with shiny shells."

The two men sat in silence, watching the young mother and child. She offered another word to the dog and talked and hummed to her baby.

"A courageous little thing," said MacLeod. "Shows no fear in a camp full of men, even after her past experience."

Rojo nodded. "Capable woman. Me mam was another. I'm one of twelve born to her. Had a hard time keepin' us fed, but we helped. Easy to halve the potato if there's love. Me dah wasn't good for much 'cept makin' babies. This poor one has had no one but 'erself to count on, but she comes from an important family."

Red Sky returned Little Leaf to the board and glanced at the men, then wrapped the blanket around herself and the babe and turned her back on them. No fear of being surprised with that odd-eyed protector at her feet.

"She'd be recognized as a woman of wealth among her people, Cap'n. The olivella shells she wears are money and the otter skins show her status. Women own the houses. A bad husband can find himself out in the cold."

Gregor frowned. He didn't need this complication—a woman in hunting camp. "The thing now is, what'll we do with her? She won't want to sleep in the cabin with the six of us. The hunters are still half-scairt of her and may try to harm her. I foresee a long night. Naught we can do but make her a bed out here. Time enough to see to a house of her own tomorrow."

The men prepared to turn in. No amount of persuasion could induce Red Sky to enter the cabin, so MacLeod shared another of his blankets and built a bough bed for the young woman near the fire. He and O'Shea reassured her with the words they had, but she would not leave the rock until they went inside.

"Let's leave her, Rojo. I ken she prefers her own company. If it rains, mebbe she'll come in." MacLeod added another chunk to her pile of firewood and spread his bed in the doorway of the cabin. To get to her, a man would have to go over him.

He left the door ajar and watched Red Sky. She donned the shirt and rolled up the sleeves. It hung almost to her shins. She stretched one blanket on the rough bed and laid bairn and board on the boughs, then covered the babe and herself with the other. Pachu settled, nose between his paws, facing the cabin.

MacLeod wished he were beside Red Sky—and not only because he missed his blankets. He couldn't forget the feel of her. Softness that stirred him as he hadn't felt for a time. Spirited and comely. Aye, a woman for any man.

He sighed. He had a duty. He'd act according to God's Word.

Sleep ye a bit, lassie.

Red Sky tugged Little Leaf's board nearer beneath the covering and freed the baby's arms and legs from the swaddling. Little Leaf stretched and yawned. The fire glowed its comfort.

A wild ending to the day. What should she do? The native hunters could not be trusted, but instinct told her these light-skinned men were not like the others. She need not fear them. Even before she saw the Russians and Aleuts, she'd felt mistrust. There was no caution now. No visions of danger.

These men seemed to want to help, though she needed none. She was strong and able to care for her baby. Still, they offered a strange comfort. She had been alone for so long. She could always run. She'd been careless in her curiosity to see the one that had ventured from camp to the north end. The island offered many secret places, including sea caves that one must enter from underwater. They wouldn't find her again if she chose to hide.

"Sleep, my sweet one, at your mother's side," she whispered. "Safe and warm." Little Leaf yawned again and closed her eyes.

The new day would be time enough to decide whether to stay with the men. Red Sky would rest, warm and prepared. She touched the knife at her waist. A light sleeper, and she had Pachu. She wouldn't be taken unaware.

Twenty-Two

The faint fingers of false dawn lit the sky as MacLeod stepped out the door. Red Sky was at work. On the far side of the fire, her baby on her back, she set several planked fish to catch the heat and smoke of the freshened fire. They'd be ready by evening. Leftovers for breakfast roasted on embers at the outer edge of the blaze.

Pachu snarled a warning, and MacLeod approached with care. Red Sky clicked her tongue and the dog settled. She pointed to the fish. "*Kalul,*" she said.

"Kalul," he repeated and reached for the dipper. "I make drink." He kept the fire between them as he brewed the tea. Stirring two spoonsful of sugar into her cup, he offered it. She made a face, but he tipped the cup toward his mouth and held it out again. "Good."

Her face lit when she took a sip. Touching, her delight with the sweet taste. She turned and the baby girl peered up at him and blinked.

No whimpers. Must have been fed. Good little thing, he mused. He remembered a lot of bawling when his brothers were bairns.

When the hunters emerged, they eyed Red Sky, their mistrust etched on their faces. She backed away as the men muttered among themselves.

"Red Sky cooked your breakfast," Rojo told them and took a big bite of warmed-over fish. They dug in.

As they ate, MacLeod said, "Tell her of the cache of staples inside the cabin."

Rojo shook his head. "She could filch it and disappear. I need me sugar. Keep me tobacco in a hidey-hole but I'd miss me sugar."

MacLeod lifted his chin in her direction and O'Shea ambled over. They were at it a while and MacLeod went to see what the talk was about. "She says it's time for the ceremony."

"Ceremony?" MacLeod's curiosity was piqued.

"Before her people hunt, it must be done. To recognize the worth of the prey's life, be it plant or animal."

Rojo sneezed. "Sorry, Cap'n." He rubbed at his nose. "In her mind everything has power. All move in a cylinder of life and death and any point in the circle is as important as any other. Animals and people and plants—all life equal in importance."

He arranged the hunters in a line and motioned for MacLeod to join them. They faced the rising sun.

Red Sky stood facing them and began a chant, then turned her back. Off came the shirt. She faced the sun, bending and swaying, as her voice rose and fell. Her arms moved from side to side above her head. The shells in her hair chattered and sparkled.

MacLeod could not take his eyes off her. *Lovely. Graceful and confident. A verra special woman.* "The hunters are settling," he whispered to Rojo.

"Familiar ceremony. They recognize she's exercising her right as a chief's daughter. Mebbe a visionary. Follow her lead and she'll become more trusting of us."

The ceremony finished, Red Sky and the baby disappeared in the direction of the creek. The hunters had a skinning and drying operation near the beach, so the men would not return until evening. Then they'd find time to build her a better shelter.

MacLeod thought of Red Sky several times during the day. Would she still be in camp? When the day was finished, he hurried ahead of the others.

There she was by the big rock, working on a small brush hut, bairn on her back, and knife at her waist. Pachu lay near a rough travois.

Looked like she'd returned to her former shelter and brought what she needed for the framework of this one. Bent saplings were tied together with strips of leathery reeds, and other limbs interwoven to form a strong foundation. The hut was perhaps eight feet in diameter, less in height. A cone shape with a blunt apex, its doorway was so small that even Red Sky would be forced to bend.

"Help her." MacLeod ordered as he began stripping brush.

Rojo and a couple of the hunters joined in. They soon had it covered and stood back. Red Sky looked pleased as she carried objects from the travois.

Outside the doorway she placed her implements for harvesting the sea. MacLeod recognized digging and prying sticks for unearthing clams and oysters, pack baskets, and sacks finely woven of sea grass. A fish spear had a point of what appeared to be a sea elephant tooth.

MacLeod shoved two large baskets just inside the door where she pointed. The largest contained dried abalones, perhaps a hundred them, and the other held small, silvery fish, dried and shrunken to the size of a finger. Still another held what Rojo called her remedies, small bundles of dried plants, bark, and twigs.

She took her bow and lance inside. Close at hand if she needed them in the night. Red Sky stood and surveyed her hut, then turned to the men. "Good," she said in clear English and smiled the most beautiful smile.

MacLeod's heart skipped a beat. He grinned from ear to ear and Rojo muttered, "Careful, Cap'n. She's still a woman. Stubborn and set in her ways, as they all are."

MacLeod brought an oiled canvas and Rojo explained it was for the floor of her hut. The shelter was as weather-tight as they could make it. He addressed the hunters. "None of us will enter. It is the home of Red Sky and Little Leaf."

"A good sign o'er yestere'en, Rojo. Wasn't sure she'd stay." He hoped she'd remain with them, snug and safe. But he knew little of her kind. She might take offense and disappear. He had no doubt she could avoid them as she'd eluded the Rooskies.

Red Sky picked up a cupped stone and laid three of the silvery fish in it, went to the fire, and lighted them. The oil in them flared. The hut offered a comforting glow each time MacLeod looked out in the night. It warmed his heart to think of Red Sky and Little Leaf snug inside.

Red Sky began working alongside MacLeod and the hunters, day after day, the baby always on her back. The bairn's calm nature was impressive. Her little face was all that showed from swaddling laced to the board, and her lively eyes seemed to miss nothing. Little Leaf watched, offering only a whimper when she was hungry. Red Sky left the men to nurse her and allow the bairn to nap. Sometimes MacLeod could hear the mother singing to her baby girl.

After a week, Pachu left the camp. "To join his wild brothers," Red Sky told Rojo. Occasionally, the dog came to her at the camp and she fed him, but she did not try to make him stay. "All animals and people are free," she said. "Do not tie them."

Red Sky enjoyed working alongside her new clan. Preserving otter skins was woman's work, but these men worked with her. Each skin had to be laced onto a drying frame made of two stout poles. They met at the nose of the animal and stretched apart at the hind legs. The forepaws were held out by short sticks and the broad tail was stretched and corded in place.

She worked faster than any of the men, and they began to copy her methods. One of the hunters told her he was happy no husband came with poisoned arrows. Red Sky smiled until she remembered why Achak would never protect her again.

The first one up each day, she nursed Little Leaf. Then it was her duty to encourage the sun to rise into the sky. Ceremony finished, she started first food for the men. The golden-haired chief helped her. She and the chief were the last to leave the skins at night, removing from the frames any that were cured. So different from men of The People.

After a time, she began to worry. Why did the white men want so many? Their tribe must be enormous, with a huge number of important people. How many *osses*, chieftans and visionaries did they have?

They observed the ceremony required before hunting. Their hunters were men of the mission, not strange men of the North. They were careful and respectful of the lives they took, never taking female otters with pups on their chests. The light-skinned men of her new clan had strange ways, but they provided much food.

One morning Red Sky stayed behind. When she was alone, she carved the shape of her hand into the big rock of the campsite. The rock had memory. Anyone who came to the island could put his hand within the carved outline and recall Red Sky's existence and the memories and wisdom of all the people she'd encountered. Ones yet to come would learn from the rock. Her people would not be forgotten.

Red Sky added a woman's touch MacLeod had missed. She was a marvel. Never idle. She foraged for foods to supplement their usual fare. She gathered roots and nuts and berries, and ground them into tasty fare or stewed them with some of the dried abalones. One evening she brought a clutch of eggs and showed Rojo a spread of Harlequin ducks bobbing on the pounding surf. They feasted for the next two days.

She learned how to use the iron kettle that hung over the flames and showed MacLeod and Rojo how she cooked by dropping heated rocks into a water-tight basket. A *tsila*, she called it. In it, she made her sea food stews. It was lined with pitch from the water's edge, but MacLeod couldn't detect a tarry taste.

MacLeod found he liked kelp if it was picked young and prepared right. When Rojo tired of fish and killed another goat, he showed Red Sky how to cook underground in a pit of coals.

Red Sky's cleanliness and modesty were inspiring. Her simple dignity commanded MacLeod's respect. He smiled, thinking of his shirts. He'd given her two. She still ignored the neckline button so the shirts hung open to her mid-section, but it was better than the shell ropes. He'd had trouble with those shells.

Every evening she washed the shirt of that day and put on a clean one. She persuaded MacLeod and Rojo to change when they bathed, and laundered theirs along with hers. The camp was rarely without linen shirts draped on shrubs.

MacLeod could lose himself in Red Sky's large, expressive broon eyes and his fingers itched to touch her shiny black hair and feel those shells. Her somewhat flattened nose melted into flaring cheekbones. She was fairer than many he'd seen. Living on the tree-shaded island, she showed only a golden tan. He remembered old ones of coastal tribes whose skin darkened to gray after years of sun exposure.

He wondered if Rojo struggled with attraction as he did. Women had been rare in MacLeod's life. He wondered if Red Sky ever had thoughts of him as a man, but his respect for her stopped him in his tracks. She trusted him. A powerful deterrent. Made him want to protect her.

He began to look forward to evenings before bedtime when she consented to sit with him and O'Shea at the fireside. One evening Red Sky removed Little Leaf from her board and laid her in MacLeod's arms. He was pleased to be chosen over Rojo. He rubbed along the baby's back. She arched until her little face was red and offered happy grunts.

"Feels good, eh?" He rubbed her soft cheek with one big finger. "Bonnie lassie," he crooned. "Who's a sweet lass, then?"

Little Leaf's fingers curled around his. She kicked her feet and smiled up at him. His heart swelled and he looked at Red Sky. She favored him with a sweet smile.

Rojo sat watching them, shaking his head and grinning. They worked at language for a time. MacLeod learned a few new words of Red Sky's dialect and she practiced English words. "Gray-gorr," she said in faithful imitation of his Scottish burr. He nodded encouragement. "Ro-ho. Ret Sky. Lee-tul Lee," she enunciated, pointing to each in turn.

He caught her slender, tapering fingers into his broad hand and treasured it for a moment, then raised his gaze to her face. "Lit-tle Leaf," he corrected, stressing the *f*.

She said something in her language to Rojo. His answer made her face set in disappointment.

"Wants to know what we do with the skins. I told her we sell them for much money. She says it's wrong to kill unless you need the animal. I told her we need the money, but I don't think she likes it."

After that conversation, Red Sky no longer helped the hunters. She stayed to herself and MacLeod feared she might leave, thinking he and Rojo were no better than the Rooskies.

MacLeod respected her choice. The otters were sacred to her and she would not aid in their slaughter. But, after a week, he found Red Sky again at the morning campfire cooking for the men. She refused to go near the otter skins, or speak of them, but she must have worked it out in her mind that MacLeod's beliefs differed from hers. He must somehow see the hunt as good or he would not do it.

Her acceptance touched him anew. She trusted him in a rare way, and her trust sank into his soul. The hunt was somehow tarnished for him—his motives now questionable.

On one of the Sabbaths toward the end of the season, MacLeod persuaded Red Sky to go kayaking with him. "Ye can bring yer wee pocket," he said, pointing to the small bag she often wore at her waist. She'd told him of several sea caves on the island, and he wanted to explore. For the *baidarka* trip, she bound Little Leaf to her chest where she could see her and protect her from jutting rocks. Red Sky proved proficient with an oar.

Their first destination was the huge cave MacLeod had seen near the narrow north end of the island. Red Sky said the sea ran through it onto the far shore. An incoming swell washed the kayakers into the darkness of the cavern and another carried them out. Deft maneuvers enabled them to avoid being slammed against its walls. The two emerged into sunlight on the far side of the island, laughing. A sweet sound, her laugh.

A sandy beach and interesting tidal pools kept them exploring for a time. At her waist, Red Sky had the pouch she'd lined with damp seaweed. MacLeod watched her add small sea animals as ingredients for one of her tasty stews.

Farther down the coast they found formations that looked like a rock garden in the sea. The explorers discovered an arch where surf had eroded away a headland, and they spotted blow holes of submerged caves. She was more relaxed away from the other men and he basked in her beautiful smiles.

Was she the one for him? She seemed to need no more talk than he did. MacLeod watched her the next evening. Graceful, yet strong. Sweet disposition. A woman to bear him sons.

What of his plan to return to Skye, marry a proper Scots lass, and regain his father's holdings? He could see Dunvegan, the austere stone stronghold of Clan MacLeod for five hundred years, with its single tower and rounded sentry rooms.

A mile away stood the plastered white stone manor of his father, with its high slate roof and multiple chimneys. Smoke curled up from small, whitewashed dependencies gathered near it, like chicks about their hen. Home, it was. He'd regain it. With a fortune in furs, it was possible. Gold coin was the key that opened any door to a determined man.

An image arose of Red Sky shivering in the gloom and rain of a Scottish winter. The dark forest closing in, so unlike the windswept coasts of California. Was it fair to try to persuade her? She was happy with her life.

Still, as he watched her serene acceptance of a meager life, he couldn't stop thinking about offering her a better one. He wanted forever, not a dalliance while he made his fortune. Had his search finally brought him to the perfect woman? Few men would agree. Rojo wouldn't.

MacLeod's attitude and ambitions had changed. Red Sky's reverence for all life had left its mark. Was it not a more Christ-like outlook than his? She couldn't understand why white men took skins to sell to other white men. Skins were not meant to make a person look good. Hers were a badge of authority and she wore them for years, perhaps a lifetime. Her shells bought only what she needed.

Because of Red Sky, MacLeod came to a new understanding as he read the Creation story for the hundredth time. God created mankind in His own image, into a relationship filled with love and respect. Being born in the image of God did not imply giving humans the right to abuse each other or any part of the creation God called good.

MacLeod was sick of killing. Was it really God's plan for his life? To profit from the deaths of some of God's most unique creations and use the wealth for retribution toward an enemy? They wasted the carcasses. Was it proper thanks to the God who rescued his soul?

What if he could persuade Red Sky? They could stay in the Californias, close to her kind. Perhaps live in the mission village. He'd build a house for her and Little Leaf and continue his sea voyages. They could go with him or remain safe at the mission.

He'd met Rojo's godly friends, Antonio and Anna Rivera. And Fray Peralta was respectful and caring of all his converts. It would work. He knew it. How could he make her see? She feared the mission, its illnesses, and the hard men. She knew little of its benefits. Her time there had been brief and traumatic when her people sickened and died. It would not be easy to convince her to give it another chance.

By the end of October, MacLeod was ready to rendezvous with the *Abagael*. He tried for a week to persuade Red Sky. Language made it difficult. He told her he wanted her leave the island with him and his men. To come with him. He would take care of her and Little Leaf.

She shook her head. "We stay. Not sick. You come."

"I make house." He pointed to her and Little Leaf. "Just you two."

She laughed and pointed. "House there."

He understood. A strong woman who could provide for herself and her child, but what if the Rooskies returned? What if she fell ill? He couldn't leave her. He wouldn't.

Two days before the rendezvous, MacLeod became desperate. "You *will* come with me. *Oloipa—* obey," he commanded.

Her face set. She turned and disappeared into her hut.

MacLeod's heart sank when he came out of the cabin next morning and Red Sky was not at the campfire. He put Rojo and the men to preparations for departure and set off toward the northern end of the island where he'd first discovered her and Little Leaf. He searched the area, but found no sign. Why hadn't he tried to make her understand how he felt about her? Would it have mattered?

Heartsick, he hurried back to camp and pulled the others from their duties. "Find Red Sky. We'll have time for the rest." But they returned in defeat.

"She'll be all right," Rojo said. "Been living on her own for a while now."

MacLeod almost hit him. He entered Red Sky's abandoned shelter. Her weapons and most of her things were missing. She did not mean to return.

Keep her safe, Father. Help me find her.

The last day. MacLeod's chest was heavy, his eyes gritty. He hadn't slept. He gave orders for the men to load the otter skins into the boat and break camp. Three native oarsmen would row the *baidarkas* out to meet the ship. With the other, he and O'Shea would transport their precious cargo to the *Abagael* in the eighteen-footer.

MacLeod pumped up his air rifle and hiked to the cave on the ridge that held the cache of extra food, praying with every step for Red Sky and Little Leaf. He'd take the cached food back to the campsite for her. Just after sunrise he sighted the large rock near the entrance. Inside, as his eyes adjusted, he caught a movement and shouldered his gun.

Red Sky crouched over Little Leaf, knife in hand. Without a word he crossed the space and lifted her and the baby into his arms. She didn't struggle as he carried them out.

He set her down, and brushed his knuckles along the smooth skin of her cheek. "Ye're going with me, darlin'. Ye're going with me and I'll keep ye safe, ye and the bairn. *Kolo, tahawiki,*" he whispered. The unfamiliar words he'd learned the night before filled his mouth like marbles. "I love you, my good wife."

Red Sky's dark eyes stared up. She put her head against his chest and MacLeod held her, Little Leaf between them. He took the babe into his arms for the trip to camp. There'd be no return to the Isle of Skye for Gregor MacLeod.

Twenty-Three

A week later, Red Sky stood beside Gregor in the church of Mission San Carlos de Borromeo. Rojo's friends, Anna and Antonio, were close by, offering support in their ability to speak the language of The People. They did not seem to find it strange that Gregor wished to marry a native woman. Anna had brought several choices for Red Sky's dress. She picked one the color of the tall pine trees growing along the crest of Far Island.

"Ye look beautiful," Gregor said, "but I miss the shells in yer hair."

"Like Anna." Red Sky pushed back the thick tresses now freed from confinement. She wished for Gregor's big shirt, or even one of the *cotónes* the *Indios* wore. Neither would pinch and rub as the dress did.

Her mind was awhirl, bombarded by the experiences of the past few days: new faces, new words, and unfamiliar food and clothing. She had not slept well in the *monjería,* crowded in among other unmarried women, even though she had her baby beside her.

The women asked questions and disturbed Little Leaf with their attentions. A few avoided Red Sky, thinking she had magic powers, and others showed disapproval of her upcoming marriage to a man not of The People.

"Don't ye worry," Gregor soothed. "Life will be lovely when we marry. Ye can wear whatever ye want in our house and invite only the people ye like."

The Gray Robe called Fray Peralta counseled the couple about the meaning of marriage in the church and about the baptism ceremony. Most of his words held little meaning, but she did understand one point. If Red Sky accepted the washing, it meant she would follow the teaching of Gregor's God, *Cristo.* She would be known thereafter by a Christian name, Dominga.

Red Sky frowned and shook her head. "Red Sky. Not Dominga."

Gregor tried to explain. "Little Leaf will be called Pía. Dominga means *of the Lord* and Pía means *compassion.*"

Red Sky shook her head again. The words made no sense.

Then he said, "The names bring us together in God's sight. The priests and I will help you learn the way of Christ."

She understood *together.* The new name must be good. She could learn the ways of Cristo if Gregor thought they were right. Red Sky wanted to be Gregor's wife, but to do that she would have to become Dominga. To take up the ways of a Spanish woman. Could she do that? She was Red Sky, the daughter of a Rumsen chieftan.

Another life called to her—one where she was

free to roam the forest, dressed only in an otter skin skirt. With Pachu beside her, she had needed nothing more. Now all had changed. The silence of the forest and the sound of the surf were gone, replaced by mission bells and the voices of many people. Her dresses scratched and chafed, the language was strange, and the food too salty. Had she made a mistake in leaving Far Island?

She remembered the comfort of Pachu beside her; running her fingers through his thick fur and the place on his chest she scratched. Gregor could help her find him. He could be with her here, encouraging her. She shook her head.

No. He is free and I am glad.

Gregor chose to live at the mission. To feel his strong arms around her brought more satisfaction even than roving with Pachu in the old, free days. She could learn new ways if they pleased her man. Red Sky smiled and nodded at the kind faces surrounding her.

Finally the wedding day arrived, bringing with it the uncertainty of two ceremonies performed by Fray Peralta. Red Sky's mouth felt dry as she watched Gregor for clues.

Anna and Antonio Rivera stood by them. Antonio held the hand of their two-year-old daughter, Aurora. The child touched Little Leaf's foot and whispered, "*Hermanita.*" Little Sister.

"*Padrinos,*" Gregor called Anna and Antonio. "Godparents. They promise to teach Little Leaf the ways of God and help her however they can."

Red Sky stared at the couple. Gregor would never let anyone take her baby from her, but it was worrisome to think of another mother and father for Little Leaf. She needed no help with her child.

The Gray Robe took Little Leaf from Gregor's arms. He held her closely, as if he had done it many times, smiling down at the baby and touching her dimpled cheek. Little Leaf showed a happy interest in her new friend, cooing sweetly.

"The servants of God, Dominga and Pía, are baptized in the name of the Father, the Son, and the Holy Spirit," Fray Peralta intoned three times as he poured baptismal waters over their heads.

The newly-christened Pía squawked a protest at the cold water and Gregor reached out for her. "Me daughter, Pía, and me wife, Dominga," he said, his eyes shining.

"Good neighbors," Gregor told her, gesturing toward Anna, Antonio, and Rojo.

New friends. The Gray Robe, Fray Peralta, was a gentle man like Gregor. Red Sky looked into Gregor's eyes and spoke the words that transformed her into Dominga, the wife of Gregor MacLeod. She had a mate; Little Leaf had a father again. *Pee-ah*, she corrected herself. Gregor would make the new life better than the old one.

He slipped a gold ring onto her slender finger. He held up her hand for all to see. "It was me mam's. She was the person dearest to me until I found you, Dominga."

Anna translated Gregor's words into Rumsen for Dominga. "He loves you more than anyone else."

Gregor twisted the ring on Dominga's finger. It glowed against the tan skin of her hand. "Never take it off. Like the ring, I will be with you forever."

When he lay with her that night in the cabin of the *Abagael*, she found his kisses strange. Touching lips? The kisses continued and she felt a stirring. When Gregor's blue eyes blazed, she understood his satisfaction with her response. She would never want another man.

⌀⌀⌀

The next morning Dominga stood beside her husband on the deck of the *Abagael*. Wind blew through her hair and filled the sails. "Wings," she said in her peoples' language, pointing upward. "White wings."

Gregor laughed. "Aye, easier than rowing a *baidarka*, eh?" He stroked her cheek. "Takes some effort to think of ye as Dominga, instead of Red Sky."

Dominga understood only every third or fourth word Gregor said, but his tone and his expression told her all she needed. Like all the words of the night before, they meant she and Pía had family again. She had a mate who cared about her.

This bright morning her man looked strong and ready. His arms lifted Pía high into the air and Dominga imagined he spoke to her of sights she would see and adventures they would share.

Pía laughed and waved her arms, as if she welcomed their new life.

The ship sailed north, loaded with the furs of the sacred otters, its crew working under Rojo's capable orders. Gregor said he would trade the furs for lumber and other valuables needed at the mission.

"I ken a Frenchman who owns a trading post just south of Maka Bay. As far from his own kind as I am from mine. Has a Maka wife. Perhaps ye'll find a friend, Dominga."

Rojo translated Gregor's words. Then added, "Ye may see all kinds of people. Pierre trades with lots of fur hunters—Brits and even Russians."

Dominga's heart hammered. "Russians? No! Bad men."

Gregor glared at Rojo. "Not likely we'll see any, m'love. Even if we do, they won't risk causing a fight and lose their trading privileges."

Russians! She stared at the sea around them. It had changed. No longer the familiar ocean that washed the shores of California and Far Island, it was the waters of the Russians. Gregor steadied the wheel. The waves loomed larger, seeming to threaten the *Abagael*. Could the evil black boat be hiding behind one of them?

Dominga held Pía close and strained to hear Gregor's words, but the only sound in her ears now was the echoing surge of the ocean beneath them. Its white lips opened and closed, waiting to swallow whatever fell into their depths.

"Pierre has a saw mill," Gregor continued, watching her face. "He'll trade our furs for wooden planks. I'll build a strong house for ye. Ye and Pía can live it as ye please."

Rojo translated and stated, "I will help him, Dominga. We will build ye a house as fine as any in the village."

Dominga smiled at the thought of her new home far away from the North and the Russians. "I gather acorns. Make *atole*."

"I like the stuff," Rojo said. "Took a little getting used to, but it can't be as good as yer seafood stews."

"I cook. You eat."

Rojo grinned. "Yes'm."

The *Abagael* finally reached the bay near Pierre's trading post. The landscape was silent—foreboding.

A dog howled in the depths of a dark forest that smothered the edges of a narrow beach. Fingers of fog slithered between the closely-packed, tall trees. Barely visible through the mist at the edge of the forest stood a cluster of log buildings—a long house and several smaller ones. No voice greeted them. Not a living soul could be seen.

"What d'ye think, Rojo?"

The Irishman shook his head. "Don't know what to make of it. In every port the natives are out in force to meet a ship. Something's wrong."

Dominga's chest tightened as she watched the men. She thought of The People's silent village after the Russians departed. "Russians kill people?"

"Not likely. But something's amiss. I think ye should go below with Pía," he said. "Rojo and I will see what is aboot at the trading post."

Through a porthole, Dominga watched Gregor row to shore with Rojo and another crew member. They disappeared into the long wooden house. It seemed an eternity before they returned.

Gregor pulled her and Pía into his arms. He stroked her long hair. She felt his reluctance to speak. Finally he whispered, "People are dying. The coughing sickness, Pierre says. Three of his children are dead."

Dominga pulled back and stared into his anxious face. "Leave, Gregor. No stay."

"Ye're safe here, but don't let Pía outside the cabin. I'll help Pierre bury his bairns. Then we'll load the planks and be on our way home."

"Leave, Gregor. Now."

"Soon, m'love. Stay inside."

At the end of the second day, the *Abagael* set sail

south for Monterey Bay. Dominga breathed easier, despite a rough sea. Gregor lured her onto the swaying deck of the *Abagael* to stand beside him at the wheel.

His head thrown back and his eyes closed, Gregor breathed deeply. "The sea-faring life. There's naught like it. Naught like the feel of wind in yer hair and the salt on yer lips." He opened his eyes. An inviting smile teased her to respond in kind.

What could she say? Dominga's stomach churned and she clasped Pía tightly. A wave washed across the deck below them. Pía squirmed in her arms and whimpered to be free.

Gregor pointed to a raft of sea otters near shore. Dominga managed a wobbly smile. Never would she want to return to the North and its hungry sea.

She could not sail on the floating house again—the ship that Gregor loved. She would wait for the right time to tell him. But tell him she must. He would be sad, but she would not give Pía to the sea.

The ocean had once been her friend and yielded its abundance to feed The People. But the northern waters beneath the *Abagael* were not the ones of Far Island. The shallows around the island were different. Nothing could hide there, but this northern sea was deep and cold, and she had no idea what lay beneath. Somewhere behind its crashing waves lurked the Russians' black bird of prey.

Dominga had never seen such a house as Gregor and Rojo built. It was near the house of Anna and Antonio. Gregor hired *indio* workmen to help as he and Rojo labored to build up double-sided walls from the redwood planks. The spaces between were filled with adobe mud, tamped down, and left to harden.

"The wood keeps the house from melting in the rain and protects it when the earth shakes. Other houses might fall, but not ours," Gregor said.

Dominga thought of her mother. She had wanted many grandchildren to comfort her in her old age, but she had not lived to see the birth of Little Leaf, or even Red Sky's marriage to Achak. What would Dukah say about her daughter's new name and her house made of wood? How would she have viewed Gregor MacLeod, a man who spoke a strange language, hunted the sacred otters, and sailed about in a floating house with wings?

Gregor built a bed for the new house. It was large and soft, but instead of comfort, Dominga found torment each night after her husband slept. When she closed her eyes, she could see the *Abagael*. Waves washed the deck, threatening to sink the ship and take Pía and Gregor from her. Floating nearby was the black boat of the Russians with its red face and hooked beak.

After many nights, she woke Gregor one morning before *ismén* showed its face. "I not go with you on the sea. Pía crawls. Wave swallow."

"I'll make a little harness to strap to her waist. Ye can hold onto her."

Dominga shook her head. "No. We stay. Safe from sea and bad men."

"You had a bad dream. The Russians are no danger, wife. Trust me to keep ye safe."

"No one safe. I see." Somewhere on the ocean, bad men sailed, waiting to pounce on the *Abagael* and everyone on it. If Gregor would not listen, at least she could save Pía.

Gregor cradled her chin in his fingers and sighed a frustrated sound. "All right, m'love. Ye and Pía stay here in our little house. Anna and Antonio are near to help. I'll sail without ye. But I'll return as soon as I can to be with the women who own me life."

Twenty-Four

Dominga found much to like about her new life at the mission—with one exception. The bells. When they woke her one morning, she turned to Gregor and said, "No like bells."

He was up on one elbow, his face close to hers. He smiled and said, "I like watching you sleep. You are so beautiful."

Red Sky laughed. "Love you, too. Talk of bells."

"Determined little thing, aren't you? All right. We'll talk about the bells. They call us together. Come with me after mass. I want to show you something."

Later, Pía in Gregor's arms, they walked to the mission quadrangle. A stone sundial on a pedestal occupied its center. Carved around the edge of its face were figures of people doing different activities.

"The iron stake casts its shadow in different places around the dial during the day. It is now on the figure of a man working. It is time to do the chores. In a few hours it will move to the one of a man sleeping. Then it will be time for people to eat and rest. The bells tell what the sundial shows. It helps people live and work together."

Dominga's face set. "No need bells. I know when to eat or work."

Gregor laughed. "It's different for ye. As my wife, ye need to listen only for the bell in the morning calling us to prayers, and the Angelus in the evening bringing us together for more prayers."

Dominga wrinkled her forehead and gave an impatient huff.

"Bells ring, people run. Not good."

"Choose to work with others if you want. Anna enjoys helping in the school. You might enjoy cooking, gardening, or helping at the hospital. You have some good herbal remedies."

"Maybe," Dominga said. Foolish, the bells. What kind of people had to be told when to eat or sleep?

Aside from the bells, much about mission life pleased her. Pía played endlessly with Aurora and was learning to speak in Spanish, as well as the English of her father and the native words of her mother. With Anna's help, Dominga sewed a shirt for Gregor and loose dresses for herself and Pía.

Proud to show the home Gregor built, Dominga welcomed Antonio and Anna, along with *Presidio Comandante* Juan Uribe and his wife. Fray Peralta visited often. On one visit he brought flower seeds and allowed Pía and Aurora to help him plant them near the front door.

"Plant and not eat?" Dominga asked. But the flowers looked pretty and Gregor and Pía liked them.

Fray Peralta talked to her of the God *Cristo*. This God did not seek vengeance even on the people who killed his Son. Instead, He invited the murderers to believe in Him and live with Him forever. Dominga was not sure she wanted to live forever with the Russians who had killed Achak and her father.

Happy days. She did not think of Far Island often, but all too soon, Gregor said, "I must return to the sea. Are ye sure ye won't sail with me?"

"Pía and I wait for you here."

The next morning, Dominga stood with Anna and Antonio on the sand as Gregor set sail. Fray Peralta and many people of the mission were there. They waved until the *Abagael* was a speck on the horizon.

Dominga's heart was a rock within her. She carried Pía into their fine home and locked the door behind them, dreading the coming of a night without Gregor beside her.

Near her own bed, she placed the little one he had made for Pia. When the baby closed her eyes that evening, Dominga snuffed the candles and settled into an uneasy sleep. Some time later, in the darkness, the hiss of a hundred snakes filled her bedroom. Through a fog she saw Gregor aboard the *Abagael*, sailing atop a black ocean. The hiss became a roar and the sea rose to consume Gregor and his ship.

Dominga woke with a start. She looked over at Pía, reassured by the relaxed hump of her daughter tangled in the covers. Staring out her window into the dark, Dominga clasped her knees to her chest, rocking back and forth, waiting for *ismén* to show his face.

At first light, Dominga rushed the still-sleeping Pía to Anna's house. Dominga poured out her fears. "Anna, what if sea takes Gregor?"

"We'll pray to God for his safety. When the dream

comes, you must pray to *El Señor*. He will send the dream away." They prayed together, and Anna made breakfast, teaching her more about *Cristo*.

Dominga returned to her cabin. She pried up two wide floor planks in her bedroom and lifted the sea chest Gregor had filled with her treasures. Donning her deer skin cape and otter skin skirt, she searched until she found the small stone box. Inside were hairs from a coyote.

Dominga took three of them, placed them in the lid of the box, and lighted them. She chanted and prayed to Coyote, whose magic was the strongest of all. Two gods were better than one. Gregor should be safe. The dream did not return.

At the end of his first year of marriage, MacLeod was a happy man. Dominga could speak many words in English and in Spanish, as well as the dialect of her mother. Aurora and Pía were inseparable. Antonio and Anna had become treasured friends. Unselfish, godly people who made life a joy.

Making a fortune no longer appealed to him. "I want only enough money to do God's work and care for me family. The killing is over. I want to earn me living from the land," he said to Fray Peralta. "Ye're an enterprising man. Any ideas?"

Friar Peralta looked thoughtful. "As a matter of fact, I have been thinking about constructing a fulling mill. Are you familiar with the work?"

"I ken the process softens wool fibers so they can be combed and woven into fabric."

The padre had a book that illustrated how a mill

worked. He pointed out the various components. "You can carve the wooden paddles and our stoneworkers can carve a millstone."

They walked to the site Fray Peralta had in mind. The waters of a creek that emptied into the Carmel River would power the mill. Its huge paddles would pound and soften fibers of woolen fabric as it soaked in a mixture of fuller's earth and water. On the side of a nearby hill lay a deposit of the necessary mineral.

Gregor's heart soared as he left the consultation on a late December day of 1788. The padre assured him the mill would earn a good profit. Besides the mission flocks, several of the big ranches in the area kept sheep, including the huge Rancho de Montaraz. All brought their wool to the mission for weaving.

He left the church office of Fray Peralta after the business plan was set and made his way to his snug little house, testing his happy plan by speaking aloud.

"Let Rojo captain the ship. He can have the thrills and adventures of the sea, and I can operate the mill." It sounded right. MacLeod had found his woman and now he wanted to enjoy her company.

"Me satisfaction is in the arms of Dominga and the thrill of watching Pía grow." He grinned. "And mebbe the joy of sons." He walked a little faster. "May as well get to work on the son project right noo."

By the end of summer, the fulling mill operated and earned a profit. The *Abagael* plied the coastline north and south with Rojo at the helm, laden with woolen fabric and dried beef. Spanish seamen carried boatloads from Monterey to New Spain. Dominga was ready to deliver a child. Pía was a happy toddler with two doting parents.

Life in *Alta California* was good for a man with the grit to make a go of it. Scotland was far away and long ago. MacLeod had achieved his dream.

But as a Scotsman, he knew that life had a way of snaking about in unforeseen twists and turns. He would remain alert to hidden reefs within his sea of contentment.

He said to Rojo one night, "Threat will one day come from the sea. Many nations have their eyes on the prize of the Californias, and Spain cannot protect them. But we need not fear—we are resourceful men."

The birth of Dougal in late September completed MacLeod's joy. God had blessed him with a healthy son and a beautiful little daughter who toddled around spreading happiness. Dominga seemed settled into life at the mission, using her spare time to help at the hospital. Life could not be better.

"I no longer need to sleep with one eye open," he said to Antonio. The men laughed together. "Perhaps there is such a thing as a perfect life on this earth. Ye ken?"

"I think we need to be grateful for every minute. Life is sometimes good and sometimes not, but God is always good. Anna and I no longer think of another child. It is in God's hands. We have Aurora."

Within a month, Rojo fell critically ill with influenza. Each day Dominga and Anna took food to him. Gregor and Antonio took turns staying with him at night. Dominga dosed him with her strongest herbs, but they had little effect on the cough or the high fever. After a week, he still showed little sign of improvement.

In one of his lucid periods, Gregor said to him, "What do ye think, mate? Are ye able to make the voyage?"

"If ye can wait another week or so, I'm yer man. But right now, I can hardly walk across the room. Seems I improve and then fall back. Bad stuff I have."

"Not sure we can wait. We have a full cargo. An English schooner is due at Maka Bay any time. They want all the cloth and beef we can provide. Can't miss an opportunity like this. Ye'd better stay here, and I'll make the voyage."

"Too weak to argue," Rojo admitted.

MacLeod's mind churned as he headed for home. Dominga would verra unhappy. The northern sea became her enemy after it brought the Russians to Far Island. She imagined horrors waiting to happen. The safe voyages he and Rojo had completed counted for little in her mind. Gregor had to make her realize her fears were unreasonable. This would be his last voyage aboard the *Abagael*; he wanted her with him.

After he had explained why he must captain the voyage, Dominga said, "I see bad things. Do not go."

"Come with me, darlin'. Ye'll be me good luck. Me last voyage. I promise. I want ye to ken the good side of the ocean life. I want me son and daughter to see it through my eyes. I'll keep ye safe. No big waves. We'll stay closer to the shore than last time. I need me family beside me, wife. A memory for me old age."

"Dougal is too young. It will not stay with him. Even Pía will not remember."

"I will. I'd not ask if I didn't believe it was safe."

"I know, Gregor. I will think on it."

Three days later, the *Abagael* departed northward

with Captain Gregor MacLeod and his family on board.

❦

A week later, Antonio woke with a start. What had broken his sleep? Thunder? He snuggled closer to Anna in the chill of an October dawn and peered at her lovely face. He thanked God once again that this beautiful, high-born woman had become his wife.

The next boom awakened Anna. "Thunder?"

Antonio grabbed his clothes. "Cannons. Come with me, *querida*. You and Aurora will be safer at the mission."

He peered out the window. Dawn's light showed two ships at anchor in the bay. One, close in, was shelling the village. Unbelievable. Who were these men?

Antonio left Anna and Aurora with the padres and hurried to the fort, anxious to learn *Comandante* Uribe's take on the danger. He and Uribe watched a cannon ball shatter the roof of an officer's quarters nearby.

"*Piratas*," Uribe declared. "They slipped in under the cover of last night's fog and refused to identify themselves throughout the night."

"Why haven't you blown them out of the water?" Antonio cringed as another ball smashed into a wall not twenty feet away. Near the shore, two small Spanish cannons answered fire, but the fort's big guns stood silent.

"The frigate doing the shelling is too close in. Our twelve-pounders can reach nothing but the top of its sails. The other is out of range." He handed his spyglass to Antonio.

"Looks like a French flag," Antonio said,

returning the glass.

Uribe nodded. "They'll be carrying *letres de marque* from that scoundrel Louis Sixteen. *Corsaires*, he calls them, but they're nothing but licensed pirates."

Pirates? Antonio could scarcely believe his ears. European conflicts were on the other side of the world.

Uribe muttered an oath. "Letters of marque should be outlawed by all, but our own government profits from the same shameful arrangement." He stared out to sea. "They raid for the crown and share in the spoils of the ships and settlements they pillage."

He raised his glass again and watched for several moments. "I set up the emplacement of small cannons during the night. They are having some effect."

The shore cannons had inflicted substantial damage near the pirate frigate's waterline. Antonio breathed a sigh of relief when it raised a white flag, then watched in disbelief as the damaged side of the raiders' ship began tilting high out of the water. "Is it sinking?"

"They've pushed their cannons and cargo to the undamaged side," said Uribe. "They'll disembark on the lowered side out of reach of our guns."

Within a few minutes a flotilla of small boats rowed swiftly for the middle of the bay, unscathed by Spanish fire. The men were pulled up into the security of the larger frigate, anchored out of range of either gun emplacement.

Comandante Uribe shook his head. "Pray, my friend. Truth is, we cannot keep them from overrunning us. They probably outnumber us ten to one. I have only fifteen men. The Spanish Crown did not foresee pirates. They worried about a few native peoples, armed with primitive weapons."

"Who would believe pirates could be so bold as to raid the Californias?" Antonio was praying for ideas. Better to think of possibilities than to worry.

"The raiders will move down the coast to come ashore. We must abandon the fort. Inform the padres that no one is safe."

"We can fort up at Rancho de Montaraz," Antonio said. "Don León can arm a hundred men."

In Fray Peralta's open carriage, Antonio and Anna stopped for nothing, fleeing with Aurora in her mother's arms. Behind them, on a pallet in the wagon driven by a vaquero, lay Sean O'Shea, delirious with the fever of a relapse. The mission's only doctor was beside him. The padres and mission inhabitants formed a ragtag army behind the vehicles, driving goats and milk cows before them. *Vaqueros* drove the mission's horse herd toward the safety of Rancho de Montaraz. The commander and few soldiers of the fort worked in vain to maintain order among the panicky people.

Confusion and the dust from many hooves and people's feet filled the air. Aurora said, "Papá, I am afraid! Why are we running away from our home?"

"We're going to a place of safety. No one will hurt you. I will be nearby."

Anna said, "Thanks be to the Holy Father that Gregor took this voyage in O'Shea's place. He's safely away on the *Abagael* and his family with him."

Antonio grunted agreement. "The bad men of the sea that Dominga fears are now a real threat, but she is not here to face them."

Aurora said, "Bad men? Who are they, Papá? Why do they want to hurt us?"

"You are not to worry, *niñita*. God is with us and

I will always be near. With the vaqueros of the ranch, we'll have an army large enough to discourage any pirates."

Twenty-Five

At the ranch, Antonio stopped to talk to Don León's new *caporal* Ricardo, and then ushered Anna and Aurora into the strongly-built barn to shelter with padres and the other women. Aurora asked permission to join some of her friends playing in the barn.

Anna held onto Antonio's arm as he sought to leave. "Don León must not see Aurora. She looks so much like him."

The cause of Anna's anxiety was valid. He was a powerful man, well able to persuade church and courts if he wanted his daughter. Fray Serra, their protector, was dead. And the governor was not a friend of the church.

Antonio took Anna's hand and raised it to his lips. "Be at ease. Ricardo says León is with his wife and sons in the house. I don't think Juliana will allow him to leave her side. Perhaps his adopted sons have satisfied León's obsession with an heir."

"But lineage is so important to him, and Aurora shares his blood." Furrows lined Anna's lovely face.

Antonio took her in his arms and kissed the top of her head. "I believe the pirates will keep León's mind away from his fixation for now. We can only leave this in God's hands, *querida*. I must join the *vaqueros*, but I will be near if you need me."

Indios of the mission strung their bows and readied their arrows. They joined Don León's well-armed *vaqueros* and *Comandante* Uriba with his few presidio soldiers behind the hacienda's wall.

Uribe turned to Antonio. "Pray, friend. I have always heard God answers the prayer of a truly good man."

By the end of the day, they had God's answer: a skirmish, in which a single soldier was killed. It seemed the *corsaires* had no stomach to face hundreds of men armed with guns and bows. And, happily, Don León had not shown his face.

Antonio constructed a makeshift tent for Anna and Aurora in the corner of the barn. "Just in case León decides to check on things out here. Ricardo says Juliana fears disease among the mission people. I don't think León will want to mix with them."

The *corsaires* moved their frigates back to the bay. Antonio and Fray Peralta followed along the shore and watched from concealment as they turned their fury on the fort. The abandoned presidio was destroyed and burned. The raiders buried the Spanish cannons barrel down in the sand and fired them.

"An act of spite." Fray Peralta pointed to the yet-undamaged mission. He formed the sign of the cross. "God protects it."

Antonio stayed on his knees with the good friar. If the pirates set fire to fields and stole or killed the remaining livestock, the settlement faced a winter of starvation. They'd probably have to abandon the site.

❧

For two days, while their ship underwent repairs, the pirates looted unhindered. Their captain set up temporary headquarters in the chapel while his men pillaged and burned officers' houses near the fort.

"We must go under a white flag and speak to the leader of the pirates," Fray Peralta said to Antonio. "God has revealed to me that his mother was a devout woman who left a trace of humanity on his soul. He will not harm us."

Antonio and Fray Peralta were allowed to enter the mission after they explained their mission to sentries. They found the pirate captain, feet on the dining table, eating and drinking wine amid the spoils. His surprise was obvious, but he motioned Antonio and the friar nearer.

"Apollinaíre du Basile and my first mate, Pierre Trouaine. You are a courageous man to seek me out, *capellán*. Your boldness pleases me. I will hear what you have to say."

Fray Peralta acknowledged the introductions with a nod. "Your words are those of an educated man. I believe you possess of a certain morality, *Capitaine*—a sense of fairness not uncommon in men of the world. I appeal to you on that basis. Please do not harm the mission or the houses of the *indios*. We offer you the contents of the storehouses, asking only that you not fire the fields. We need them to survive."

"My men are displeased with the profits. We expected ships in the harbor, a rich store of furs—and women."

The friar's expression did not change. "I can offer only the excellent wines and brandies of Mission San Carlos. We are a poor people."

"*Le diable* take that mutinous crew. They are never satisfied." Du Basile tossed his long, black curls. "Your request is granted. Go in peace, *capellán*."

By the following day, the damaged ship was repaired and Apollinaíre's disappointed crew was under way. Their ships had almost cleared the bay when a single merchant ship entered from the north. The pirate frigates turned and the murderous guns of both *corsaire* ships raked the merchant schooner's decks. Most of its crew fell in the opening assault.

After the looters boarded, Apollinaíre du Basile needed only his light saber to run through a man who crouched over his woman and children, his empty pistol on the deck beside him.

As the man lay dying in the Indian woman's arms, the pirate stood over her, wiping blood from his blade onto his victim's shirt. Then he replaced it in the ornate leather scabbard hanging at his side. He allowed her time to hear the final breath of her man and to close his eyes. She did not cry.

Comely and courageous. I might keep her with me for a while.

Dominga pressed her lips to Gregor's, holding their dead son and Pía cradled between them. She held up the hand with the gold ring Gregor had placed there at their wedding. "I love you forever, my husband."

The bad men of the sea have taken my family again. How can it be?

Gregor whispered, "Don't be afraid. God is with ye, m'love." He breathed his last.

At least she had been allowed to remain with him long enough to bring a final blessing with her kiss—to be the last thing his loving eyes beheld.

Dominga died with her husband. It was Red Sky who looked up at the *pirata*. She allowed no expression on her face as she stood, one arm around Pía, the other holding Dougal. Pía stared up at her, her bewilderment plain.

"Do not speak, little one," Red Sky said in English. "Show no fear."

"Is she yours?" du Basile growled, pointing toward Pía.

Red Sky nodded, able to understand the words he spoke in French-accented Spanish.

"You can do nothing for this one," the pirate said as he tore Dougal from her arms and tossed him onto the deck, " but I, Apollinaíre du Basile, will take the *petite fille*."

Red Sky bent and placed Dougal on his father's chest, with Gregor's arms holding his son. She offered no resistance as du Basile pulled her and Pía down the steps to quarters below.

At his orders, she brought food and drink to him and several of his men. Standing near the bunk where she placed Pía, she watched the revelry as the *corsaires* celebrated the rich store of furs aboard the *Abagael*. She refilled tankards and deftly avoided grasping hands without murmur.

246

When the others at last reeled from the cabin, the drunken du Basile turned his attention to Red Sky. Smiling, he held out a necklace and said, "A pretty jewel for a pretty woman."

Pulling her into his arms, he raised her face to his—just as the blade of the small knife from her pocket entered his heart. Shock glazed his features and he slumped to the floor, staring up at her. He raised an arm as if to seize her foot, which had begun pressing on the knife. She stood expressionless, looking down into his eyes.

For a moment it appeared he would form a word, but Apollinaíre du Basile had nothing to say to Red Sky or to any living soul upon the earth. Red Sky retrieved her small knife and wiped it upon the shirt of her husband's murderer before laying it on his reddening chest. She wanted the pirates to have no doubt who had wreaked vengeance on their leader.

Stepping out of her slippers, Red Sky unfastened her dress and petticoat and allowed them to pool on the floor of the cabin. Clad only in her chemise, she picked up Pía and slipped, wraithlike, over the side of the ship. Soundlessly she paddled toward the shore. Carrying her child alternately upon her back and floating with her daughter on her chest, it took her an hour to reach the beach.

On the sand, her arms wrapped around Pía, Red Sky lay exhausted. Even the sweet feel of her child next to her could not ease the pain—or the bewilderment. She had to think.

Why had she allowed Gregor to persuade her to go? He said it would be his last voyage and he wanted to share it with his daughter and son. She had been with him in his last moments, but if she had remained at home, their son might still be alive.

Useless thoughts. Gregor and Dougal were gone—slain by the same kind of evil men who had killed her father and Achak. Red Sky would never have another man. Once again she and Pía were alone.

Light began to paint the horizon. Red Sky led Pía through the deserted village. The town appeared to have been abandoned in haste. Doors stood open and tools were strewn about. A frightening silence lay over the town and the mission.

"Go home, Mamá. Papá and Dougal there?"

"No, they wait for us in another place. We will find food and go into the forest. There we will find family."

It would not be safe to linger in the village. The *piratas* would seek a bitter revenge on the woman who had killed Apollinaíre du Basile. Still, Red Sky was drawn to the chapel. She entered and led Pía to the altar. A strange comfort filled her as she looked up at the bleeding body of *Cristo*, the God who had died so that others might live. His eyes seemed to be looking directly at her. Her heart burned within her.

Suddenly she knew that Gregor and Dougal were with him now in that beautiful place where they would live forever. One day she would join them. *Cristo* was with her now—Gregor's dying words had told her that.

The hard men of the fort were unable to offer safety from the dangers of the sea. She must once again rely on her old ways. She would lose herself in the forest with those of her mother's people who chose not to live at the mission. There, they would be safe. She took Pía deep into the woods and put together a hasty shelter, well concealed in a ravine.

"We will rest here and tomorrow seek out kinsmen. We will have family again."

"No family. I want Papá and Dougal."

Red Sky pulled her sobbing daughter into her arms and allowed her own tears to course silently down her cheeks.

Would the body of their dead leader be buried in the open sea as Gregor said was the custom of sailors? And would the bodies of her beloved Gregor and Dougal ever be recovered from the bay?

The next morning, Red Sky sought out those of her mother's People who still lived in the wild. Leaving Pía safe in the house of her mother's brother, Red Sky concealed herself in the scrub forest of her childhood.

She watched as a party of privateers searched the wilds. Curses filled the air as the pirates slashed their way through thorny shrubs. They would not find her uncle and Pía. If they came near, The People would melt into the forest.

At the end of a fruitless day, the *corsaires* fired their pistols into the air. From the brow of a hill at sunset, she watched as the pirates sailed to the south. They took the *Abagael* with them.

Under cover of darkness, before people returned to the mission, Red Sky glided from the trees, seeking out the little timbered house she had shared so contentedly with Gregor. Its front wall had been shattered by a ship's cannon, but the raiders must have found little of interest within.

Her breath came hard and fast. Something sinister

lurked in the debris of broken planks—as if the evil of Apollinaíre du Basile crouched ready to leap upon her from the shadows. She shivered in the slimy dankness of the foggy night and hurried to finish her urgent task.

From a blanket inside Gregor's old sea chest secreted beneath her bedroom floor, she took out her sea otter skirt, her moccasins, her weapons, and her deerskin cape. She gathered all the gold coins cached in the trunk and tied them into a pillow case from the bed.

Red Sky cast off the last vestige of her days as Dominga with her chemise. Clad in the clothing of her people, she returned to the village of her mother's people.

"One more day, Uncle, I leave my daughter with you. I will make us a house of our own near the village."

"You can live here with us. We need a strong young woman to do the work of the old women of this village. Look around and see what I speak."

The huts of the settlement were a sorry sight. The tules covering them had not been replaced in many moons. Many of them had piles of bones and rotting fish just outside the doorway. There were no racks of drying meat or piles of acorns. Trash that should have been carried to a midden some distance from the houses was scattered throughout the village. Flies covered the trash, and the odor was sickening.

"Are the women sick?"

"No. We are all just old and tired. Only the *vino* of the soldiers makes us feel better. We trade the furs of animals for it."

"My father spoke against such. He said *vino* made people lazy and slow-witted."

Her uncle shrugged, then settled himself for a

rest, wine bottle in hand. "It helps my cough."

Red Sky entered the hut. Two women stared listlessly at a dying fire where a stone dish of acorn mush congealed in the ashes. She picked up Pía. "Better we sleep under the sky tonight than in this nasty place."

"Nassy, Mamma," said Pía.

What should she do? They needed the protection of family, but her mother's People no longer functioned as a family. She was once again a woman alone to fend for her child. And this time she did not have Pachu.

She did have *Cristo*. He was always with her.

Twenty-Six

Antonio was working in the pasture with two other *vaqueros* when he spotted a lone pirate hurrying toward the mission. Antonio galloped out to intercept him on the road, and led him at the end of a rope to Fray Peralta.

The *corsaire* went to his knees and begged for mercy, saying he had been forced into service on the Sandwich Islands but had finally managed to desert his murderous companions. He sought asylum at the mission.

Fray Peralta questioned the man closely. Antonio listened in anger as the deserter related circumstances of the deaths of Gregor and Apollinaíre du Basile, as well as the escape of the woman and child. But as he continued, the man's humble demeanor finally touched Antonio's heart. He found himself agreeing with the friar's judgment.

"You will remain in prison for a time while we observe your character. If you prove yourself worthy and truthful, we will allow you to live with us at the mission."

Anna, Antonio, and Rojo joined the search for Dominga and Pía. Soldiers came upon a drunken, ruined village, but the inhabitants said they knew nothing of a Dominga.

After a week, Antonio said, "Your tears will not bring them back to us, Anna."

"I don't understand, Antonio. I thought Dominga was happy here."

"She was happy here with Gregor. He was her reason for following mission life. But her real home is the forest. She is well able to take care of her child. We may never see them again."

Aurora wailed. "No, Papá. They must come back. I miss my little sister."

The whole colony joined Antonio and Anna in mourning MacLeod in a special mass celebrated for the dead: Dougal, Gregor and his crew, and the soldier from the presidio who'd been killed at Rancho de Montaraz. The friars said, "Cannons are never a solution. God is our provider and protector."

Tears dewed Anna's lashes. "Dominga should be here, Antonio. She would find comfort in the service."

"God will keep her safe, *amada.*"

When Sean O'Shea recovered from his illness, he approached Antonio. "Fray Peralta says he's talked to you 'bout the fulling mill. Says yer willin' to work with me and share the profits. Mentioned rebuilding Dominga's house for meself. I think the Cap'n woulda wished it."

"In time, you may take a wife." Antonio watched the confirmed bachelor squirm.

Rojo narrowed his eyes. "Mebbe, friend, but

don't be holdin' your breath. Let's fergit that and talk business. We'll keep the mill running and set aside a share for Dominga, in case she returns." He nodded. "And mebbe one day I'll buy a ship of me own."

"I haven't said anything to Anna, but my heart is causing pain. Fray Peralta says he recognizes the same symptoms Fray Serra suffered. He came up with this plan to get me out of the saddle."

"And to keep me fed after we lost the ship."

"He's like a *gallina*—a mother hen looking after all his chicks. He still searches for Dominga. We pray for her return every time he comes to the house."

When Red Sky left her uncle's village, she took Pía and made her way through the scrub toward the ancient place, where her father's clan had made their home before the Gray Robes came. It was a long hike over the coastal mountains. No pirate would find them. She would rebuild one of the abandoned houses and call it her own.

But when she reached the place, she found a vibrant village. She could hardly believe her eyes. The son of her father's sister stood before her. Tall and grown-up, Sacha-Mora held out his hand.

"You are welcome, Red Sky. I hope you bring us good news of your father and The People."

Red Sky had to hold back tears, thinking of all that had happened. But that was in the past. She could start again. Gregor would live through his daughter and her church name among Red Sky's people.

Sacha-Mora and The People helped her build a hut. Red Sky joined in the daily work of the women,

Pía at her side. In many ways life was like that of her childhood.

But Sacha-Mora was now the chief. He did not have Sacha-Pal's wisdom. The People quarreled among themselves, men and women. The children ran wild, undisciplined by their parents.

Pía came to her mother after a big boy shoved her into the dirt. "I do not like these people, Mamá. They are cross and noisy. Please, can't we go back to the mission?"

"Let me think about it, Pía." Red Sky gave her a hug. "Sacha-Mora's dog has puppies. He said you may have one of them. I think they are old enough to leave their mother."

"Oh, Mamá, I have always wanted a dog! What will we name him?"

"Her. We will choose a little girl dog. We will call her *Pachu-mas*. It means 'sister of Pachu.' She will be a fine companion for you and we will teach her to obey your voice. She will be happy wherever you are."

Pachu-mas was several moons old when a young man named Sanjo joined The People. He came from the mission, saying he fled when his parents died of an illness that had made many people sick. Soon after he arrived, he fell ill with the spotting sickness.

Red Sky's heart went out to him. The same illness had killed her mother. But Dukah was a woman who had lived many moons. She was married and Red Sky had been almost grown when she died. Sanjo was barely more than a boy. He must not die.

The sick young man was placed in the sweat lodge, attended by the women of the village. Red Sky brought her remedies. They made herbal teas and spooned beef broth to him when he became too weak to eat.

The *oss* brought his medicine bundle and began spreading it out.

"Will you pray with me to *Cristo*?" Red Sky asked.

"The god of the mission was not strong enough to heal this young man while he was there. I bring the curatives of The People. They are much stronger."

Red Sky hung her head. She did not have the respect of The People and their *oss* as she had on Far Island.

"I remember Sacha-Pal, your father," he said. "He had great wisdom, but you are a woman. I am the *oss*. I need no woman's help."

He unpacked sacred tools made of bone, fur, and crystal. Each evoked the spirit of the material the tool was made from. He used each tool in different ways on Sanjo's body, calling on its spirit to help him heal Sanjo.

The *oss* danced and prayed in the village center. He rubbed ashes from sacred plants over the sick man's body and passed his feathered stick over the sores. He wore his most frightening mask to scare away the demons surrounding Sanjo, and smoked his spirit pipe. The smoke would rise and bring aid from spirits of the air.

Sanjo did not improve. The *oss* burned coyote hairs in a dish and rubbed them on the sick man's lips. Then he placed his mouth over that of Sanjo, and tried to suck out the evil spirits that made him ill. Five days later, the *oss* fell sick, along with others of the village.

Two days after the death of Sanjo, sores appeared on Red Sky's neck and chest and she began coughing.

She gathered up the pillow case that held Gregor's gold. Into it she placed the stone necklace her mother had made for her. She added some dried meat and apples.

"Come, Pía. We will visit Anna and Aurora and Antonio. Bring Pachu-mas with us."

Pía clapped. "Aurora, *mi hermana.*"

"Yes, your sister. It is a long walk to their house, but I bring food for us and for Pachu-mas."

It took a full day to reach the half-way point of their journey. Red Sky said to Pía, "We will camp here under the stars tonight."

She built a fire and filled her *tsila* at a stream. As they bathed, Red Sky noticed more blisters on her arms and legs. Pía splashed in the water with Pachu-mas. They all dined on dried meat and fresh berries that Pía had picked. When they finished eating, Red Sky made beds for them on opposite sides of the campfire. The fire should burn away any harm the spotting sickness spirits passed into the air.

She tucked a blanket about Pía and Pachu-mas and said, "Tonight, I will tell you stories of the past. There is more you should know about The People who have gone before you. And you should know about Pachu, the dog who shared life with me on Far Island."

"You never told me about Pachu before, in any of your stories."

"It is time I did. Pachu was a dog like no other. I took him as a pup from a pack of wild dogs on Far Island..."

Far into the night, stories of Far Island, Pachu and Gregor MacLeod filled the minds of Red Sky and Pía. Before first light, they slept. *Ismén* was high in the sky when they arose.

Red Sky's head ached so badly it was difficult for her to see where she stepped. Her skin was hot. The sores burned and itched. As long as she was able, she spoke of the images that filled her mind, continuing the tale of Red Sky and Pachu. The rocky ground seemed to rise forever upward until she could speak no more. She needed every breath to keep moving.

Many times they stopped to rest and regain strength. It was becoming harder for her to breathe, but she urged Pía onward. Finally they struggled to the top of the tall ridge they had battled for hours.

Red Sky sank to her knees. "Look down, Pía. What do you see?"

"The mission. I see the mission, Mamá. Will Aurora be there?"

"Yes, my daughter. Your sister will welcome you. And your Godparents, Anna and Antonio. They will be glad to see you."

She saw clearly the image of Anna and Antonio standing beside her and Gregor, promising to be godparents to Pía—to provide anything she might need. It had seemed an unwelcome vow on that day.

Now Anna and Antonio would care for Pía as their own. They would teach her of *Cristo.* Pía must believe in *Cristo* and live with Him forever, just as Red Sky would. They would one day be together again— Gregor and Red Sky and Pía and Dougal—forever.

"Will we go back to our house and live at the mission again?"

"Is that what you want, little one?"

"Oh, yes, Mamá. I have missed the padres and the bells."

Red Sky laughed. "Yes, the bells." Her breath

was faint and her bones ached as if they might break with one more step. "We must go to the house of Anna and Antonio and Aurora. Let's hurry."

But the rugged, rocky way down the ridge was almost more than Red Sky could manage. She fell once and Pía cried out.

"I am good. Bring me a long stick to lean on so I do not fall again."

It was dark when they finally reached the house of Anna and Antonio.

"Knock, Pía. Knock upon the door of our good friends."

Pía knocked loudly and called, "Aurora, it's your *hermanita*. I have come back." Pachu-mas barked sharply.

Footsteps echoed in the house. Someone was running to the door. Red Sky placed the pillow case behind Pía's feet and slipped away into the night.

The End

To find out what becomes of Aurora and Pia, read the exciting sequel, *Dawn's Light in Monterey*, available wherever books are sold.

About the Authors

Marilyn Read was born and reared in cattle country. She wanted no part of the life of a rancher's wife. No saddle sores and feeding hungry cowboys in the middle of dusty pastures for her. She would read, research, and write.

She married—a rancher, of course—but she taught school, surrounded by sweet children and books. Cheryl's mother was her co-teacher and closest friend. Marilyn collected history and wrote for historical magazines and journals for sixteen years, until the day her rancher said he needed her with him more than they needed a paycheck. She finally earned her spurs.

Now a widow, she again collects history and writes historical fiction about inspired women of the southwest.

A true blue Texas girl, **Cheryl Spears Waugh** lives in the serenity of the hill country near Austin. During some of life's challenges, Cheryl discovered how faithful God is in His abounding love. Through this process grew a love for other women who have unearthed God's strength to move forward in His way.

For Cheryl, the best part of writing inspirational historical fiction is the anticipation of what is to come—standing beside women from another era who meet the challenges of a complicated life journey by discovering the joy of living close to God.

It does her soul good to be surrounded by the laughter of loved ones, an empty plate of southern home-cooking, and a page of perfectly orchestrated words powerful enough to transform the way we see the world.

God led Marilyn and Cheryl to work together in 2006, after the deaths of Marilyn's daughter and Cheryl's mother. They write about strong women in the old southwest to inspire women of today in their journey with God. *Seek a Safe Harbor* and *Dawn's Light in Monterey* are the two books of their *Women of Monterey* series.

Please visit them at Inspired Women of the South-west. **www.InspiredWomenoftheSW.com**

From the beginning, we committed our writing efforts to His hands. We required a publisher willing to accept a story about sin and forgiveness. Teresa Lynn of Tranquility Press entered our lives. We are inspired by her beautiful spirit, wisdom, and willingness to capture our vision for *Seek a Safe Harbor* and *Dawn's Light in Monterey*.

Cheryl Spears Waugh and Marilyn Read

Marilyn and Cheryl greatly appreciate all reader
feedback! Would you consider leaving a brief review
of this book on Amazon, Goodreads, or any other
book review site? We thank you!

CPSIA information can be obtained
at www.ICGtesting.com
Printed in the USA
BVHW031013050419
544725BV00001B/34/P